✦ RICHARD PAUL EVANS ✦

Lost
December

SIMON & SCHUSTER

NEW YORK LONDON TORONTO SYDNEY NEW DELHI

Simon & Schuster
1230 Avenue of the Americas
New York, NY 10020

First Simon & Schuster hardcover edition November 2011

SIMON & SCHUSTER and colophon are registered trademarks
of Simon & Schuster, Inc.

For information about special discounts for bulk purchases,
please contact Simon & Schuster Special Sales at
1-866-506-1949 or business@simonandschuster.com.

The Simon & Schuster Speakers Bureau can bring authors
to your live event. For more information or to book an event,
contact the Simon & Schuster Speakers Bureau at
1-866-248-3049 or visit our website at www.simonspeakers.com.

Designed by Davina Mock-Maniscalco

Manufactured in the United States of America

1   3   5   7   9   10   8   6   4   2

Library of Congress Cataloging-in-Publication Data
Evans, Richard Paul.
Lost December : a novel / Richard Paul Evans.
—1st Simon & Schuster hardcover ed.
p.   cm.
1. Christmas stories.   I. Title.
PS3555.V259L68   2011
813'.54—dc23   2011035082
ISBN 978-1-4516-2800-5
ISBN 978-1-4516-2802-9 (ebook)

ACKNOWLEDGMENTS

A sincere thank you to all my friends at Simon & Schuster, for all they do and have done to share my books with the world for nearly two decades.

To my Father, with love.

Lost December

A certain man had two sons:

And the younger of them said to his father, Father, give me the portion of goods that falleth to me. And he divided unto them his living.

And not many days after the younger son gathered all together, and took his journey into a far country, and there wasted his substance with riotous living.

And when he had spent all, there arose a mighty famine in that land; and he began to be in want.

And he went and joined himself to a citizen of that country; and he sent him into his fields to feed swine.

And he would fain have filled his belly with the husks that the swine did eat: and no man gave unto him.

And when he came to himself, he said, How many hired servants of my father's have bread enough and to spare, and I perish with hunger!

I will arise and go to my father, and will say unto him, Father, I have sinned against heaven, and before thee,

And am no more worthy to be called thy son: make me as one of thy hired servants.

And he arose, and came to his father. But when he was yet

a great way off, his father saw him, and had compassion, and ran, and fell on his neck, and kissed him.

And the son said unto him, Father, I have sinned against heaven, and in thy sight, and am no more worthy to be called thy son.

But the father said to his servants, Bring forth the best robe, and put it on him; and put a ring on his hand, and shoes on his feet:

And bring hither the fatted calf, and kill it; and let us eat, and be merry: For this my son was dead, and is alive again; he was lost, and is found.

Luke 15:11–24

PROLOGUE

A ninety-year-old man went to confession. "Father," he said, "I left my wife and ran off with a thirty-year-old woman."

The priest said, "That's terrible, but I don't recognize your voice. Are you a member of this parish?"

The old man replied, "No. I'm not Catholic."

"Then why are you telling me this?" The priest asked.

"I'm ninety years old," the old man replied, "I'm telling everyone."

✦

There are those who share their stories of waywardness with false shame and fond recollection—a misplaced pride in past misdeeds. I am not that fool. I share my story for your benefit, not mine. On my part, I feel nothing but shame and gratitude. Shame for the people I hurt and gratitude that they didn't desert me when I most deserved it. It has been said that sometimes the greatest hope in our lives is just a second chance to do what we should have done right in the first place. This is the story of my second chance.

CHAPTER

One

Some mistakenly believe that "prodigal" means lost or wayward.
It doesn't. It means "wastefully extravagant."
No matter, both definitions are true of me.

Luke Crisp's Diary

My seventh-grade English teacher, Mr. Adams, used to say, "No matter how thin the pancake, there are still two sides." *Two sides to every story.* People mistake that little chestnut for wisdom—as if all real evil in this world can be explained away if we'll but listen to the other side of the story. Tell that to your local serial killer. I believe that adage amounts to nothing more than moral laziness—a motto for people who carry moral compasses without needles. Make no mistake, *all* evil has its side of the story.

I'm telling you this because in presenting *my side* of the story, I do not want you to confuse it for justification. No matter what excuses I told myself at the time, my choices were wrong. I was wrong. I'll warn you in advance—as you read my story, you won't like me. I understand. Neither did I. You have likely heard the story of the prodigal son. That's my story too. I'm here to tell my side of the story.

CHAPTER

Two

Only those who never step, never stumble.

  Luke Crisp's Diary ✦

If the seeds of my fall were planted in my youth, they didn't begin to bloom until my years at Wharton business school at the University of Pennsylvania, carefully cultivated by a gardener you'll learn about later.

Before then, I lived where I was born, in Scottsdale, Arizona, an upscale suburb of Phoenix. My childhood was a little unusual. My mother died of breast cancer when I was seven, and my father threw himself into his work to deal with his grief. My father, Carl Crisp, was an innovative and brilliant man—a corporate visionary. Through his industry he built an international company. Unless you live in an Appalachian cave or a shanty in an Everglades swamp, you've probably heard of it: Crisp's Copy Centers. There are currently more than two thousand locations throughout the U.S. and Canada, the number of stores rising monthly.

My father threw himself into his work, but he didn't neglect me. Rather, he took me with him. I spent my early years at his side. When most boys my age were learning to throw a curve ball, I was learning how to replace a toner cartridge in a color copier.

By the time I was sixteen, I was managing my first copy

center—a small Crisp's copy shop in Gilbert, Arizona. I'm pretty sure that I was the only sophomore in high school driving a self-financed BMW. I oversaw twelve copy centers while going to college. By the time I was twenty-one, I had graduated summa cum laude from Arizona State University.

People always say that I look a lot like my father, which I consider a compliment. We are both tall and a little gangly, with light brown hair. But that's where our likeness ends. My father's most noticeable trait is his intense, dark eyes, partially shadowed beneath bushy eyebrows. He always told me that the secret to success is "laser focus," and he had the eyes for it. He could always see through me.

CHAPTER

On the calendar, all days look the same,
but they do not carry the same weight.

✦ Luke Crisp's Diary ✦

If I had to pick a day that my life turned, I'd peg it to six weeks after my December graduation from ASU. My father and I had been working together on a presentation and stopped to have dinner at our favorite restaurant, DiSera's, a fancy and popular Italian restaurant halfway between our home and the Crisp's corporate office building. We ate there almost weekly, and the owner, Lawrence "Larry" DiSera was a close friend of my father. We even had our own table in the restaurant, beneath a painting of a buxom Tuscan girl stomping grapes. On special occasions—birthdays and celebrations—Larry himself would come to our table and play the mandolin.

But the night my life changed, it wasn't my birthday and we weren't celebrating anything. We were just eating. Somewhere between the antipasto and the primi piatti, my father said, "I think you should get an M.B.A."

The comment came as far out of the blue as a meteor. I was glad to be back to work at Crisp's and already felt like college had been an unnecessary delay. For a moment I just looked at him. "Why?"

"I think it would be good for you."

I hoped he wasn't serious, but from his demeanor I knew he was. It was the same look he'd had when he suggested I take over as area manager of our Phoenix stores.

"I'd rather learn business in the real world," I said, "You didn't get an M.B.A. It hasn't hurt you."

"More than you think," he replied.

"You founded one of America's largest companies. How can you say it hurt you?" I punctuated my argument with a bite of caprese salad. When I finished chewing, I said, "Besides, we've got enough going on getting ready for the public offering."

"That's why I think you shouldn't wait," he said

"You want me to go back to ASU?"

"I was thinking somewhere out of state. Maybe Harvard or Wharton."

Our conversation seemed to be spiraling off in the wrong direction. "What's wrong with staying here?" I asked. "ASU's got a great business program. And there's Thunderbird."

"They're good schools," my father said. "I just think it might be good for you to get out on your own for a while. Going back East would help you get a feel for the climate outside the Southwest."

Up to that point in my life I had always lived at home with my father. "You sound like you're trying to get rid of me."

My father smiled. "Maybe I am," he said. "I've been think-ing a lot lately. It's a parent's job to give their children roots and wings. I've given you roots—maybe too many of them—but not enough wings. I think I need to nudge you out of the nest a little. I want you to fly."

"Or plummet to my death," I said.

He grinned. "That's not going to happen."

"I didn't think I was doing so bad here," I said.

"Bad? I couldn't be more proud of you. You were successfully running a multimillion dollar business at nineteen. This isn't about not measuring up. This isn't even about business. This is about your life. I want you to have the opportunities I didn't have. I don't want you to have any regrets."

"I *don't* have any regrets," I said.

He looked at me for a moment, then sighed. "Maybe I have them for you. You didn't have the childhood most of your schoolmates had."

"I don't want their childhoods. I like my life the way it is. I like working at Crisp's."

"It's a lot bigger world out there than just Crisp's."

"You don't want me to work at Crisp's?"

"I'm not saying that. You know that I want you to take over the company someday. But I want you to make that choice with your eyes wide open. It may be that in the end Crisp's is exactly what you want—or maybe it's not—but, whatever you choose, at least you had a choice. I won't take that away from you."

"If I went back East, who would take care of things here?"

"Henry will do until you get back." Henry Price was my dad's chief financial officer and number two. "I'm sure he'll relish the chance to step up."

I had no doubt he would. Henry had always struck me as ambitious. "Who will take care of *you*?"

My father looked at me and I saw a mixture of sadness

and pride in his face. "That's what I was afraid of," he said softly. "You've been watching over me instead of the other way around. I'll be fine. Besides, I've got Mary."

Mary was my father's personal assistant. She had been with my father even before my mother died—way back in the early days of Crisp's when there were just three stores and they were still running to the local office warehouse to pick up boxes of copy paper. Mary was in her late fifties, single, childless and affable. She didn't have a high school diploma, but what she lacked in scholarship she made up for in devotion to my father. I always thought she seemed more like a mother than an assistant.

My father went back to eating while I thought over his proposition. After a few minutes I breathed out slowly. "I'll think it over."

My father said without looking up, "Fair enough. In the meantime, we have the national conference to prepare for. So hurry up and eat. There's work to do."

CHAPTER

Four

*Under the right circumstances, a tiny spark
can grow into an inferno that can overcome an entire city.
So can an idea.*

✦ Luke Crisp's Diary ✦

The spark from that dinner conversation caught fire. By the next week I had sent in my application to Wharton business school. My father had an old investor friend in the Wharton administration who was able to help expedite things, and a month later my father and I were on a plane, flying to Philadelphia for my enrollment interview.

In spite of my initial resistance, I liked what I saw. I suppose that my father was right—a part of me wanted to venture out and see what else was out there. I was accepted into the program, and I enrolled with a major in operations and information management. A week after my acceptance I returned to Philadelphia to find housing. I found an apartment in Sansom Place, a tower within walking distance of the campus, and by the next August I was back in school.

Even though I was in my twenties, I was homesick those first few weeks away. It was the first time I had lived alone and Philadelphia was a strange new world. The city was crowded and old and, for most of the year, cold—a far cry from the dry heat of the Arizona desert. I had my own room in Sansom, which was a double-edged sword. The good news was that I had privacy. The bad news was that I had too much of it. Those first few weeks I was agonizingly lonely. I had no idea how much that was going to change.

My fifth week at Wharton, I was sitting in a management communications class when a pretty young woman sitting two chairs to my right, suddenly leaned toward me, her long, brown hair spilling over the vacant chair between us.

"Hi. I'm Candace," she said. She had beautiful dark, almond-shaped eyes, the kind you'd probably stare at if you knew you wouldn't be caught. I instinctively looked behind me to see if she was talking to someone else. That made her smile. "I'm talking to you," she said. "What's your name?"

"Luke," I said.

"Hi, Luke. Some friends of mine are getting together for a study group tonight at Smokey Joe's. Want to join us?"

"What's Smokey Joe's?"

"It's a local hangout. It's kind of famous. You must be new to Philly."

"Brand-new," I said.

"So am I. Want to come?"

"Yeah, sounds great."

"Good. Where do you live?"

"I'm on the fifteenth floor of Sansom Place West."

"We're neighbors. I'm on the third floor. We can meet in the lobby and walk together."

"What time?"

"Around six?"

"Great."

"Great," she echoed. She leaned back in her seat.

I found myself smiling through the rest of the class.

CHAPTER

Five

Clever people can be invigorating or draining.
Sometimes both.

 Luke Crisp's Diary

That evening I went downstairs to the lobby of my building about five minutes before six. Candace wasn't there. Around ten minutes past the hour I wondered if she was going to stand me up. I was about to go back up to my room when she came out of the elevator.

I didn't recognize her at first as she had changed her clothes. Her hair was pulled back and she wore expensive-looking denim jeans and a blue, short-waist suede jacket that accentuated her figure. She walked up to me, her face lit with a broad smile. "Sorry I'm late. My roommate came home crying and I couldn't just run out on her."

"No worries," I said. "You said this is a study group. Should I bring my books?"

She smiled wryly. "It's really not much of a study group," she said. "I don't know why we call it that. Probably so we don't feel so bad about all the time we waste. Most of us met the first weekend of preterm courses and just started hanging out." I followed her outside and we started walking west. "Smokey Joe's is this way."

The air outside was crisp and the sun was hidden beneath a canopy of low clouds.

As we walked, Candace asked, "Where are you from, Luke?"

"Scottsdale, Arizona."

"Scottsdale," she said. "Scottsdale Fashion Square."

"You've been there?"

"Several times. I love Arizona. I usually stay at the Phoenician."

"That's only three miles from my house—right by Camelback Mountain."

"I've hiked Camelback," she said. "That's a beautiful area."

"It's home," I replied. "Where are you from?"

"Cincinnati. Mostly. Growing up, my family moved a lot. But I call Cincinnati home."

"What got you into business?" I asked.

"In the words of Willie Sutton, 'That's where the money is.' "

"Who's Willie Sutton?" I asked.

"He was a famous bank robber during the Great Depression. When they asked him why he robbed banks, he said . . ."

". . . That's where the money is," I said.

She smiled. "Right."

"What's this Smokey Joe's place like?" I asked.

"You know, it's your typical college hangout. President Ford called it 'the seventeenth institution of higher learning at the University of Pennsylvania,' or something like that. They call themselves the Pennstitution. I'm not sure what that means. It's just a good place to unwind."

"It sounds fun."

"I hope it is," she said, sounding a little cautious. "I should warn you about my friends. They can be a little . . . jarring."

"Jarring?"

"Yeah, like a car accident. But at least they're not dull. They're never dull."

"That's good," I said.

"Yeah, that's good," she said. Then she added, "Usually."

✦

Smokey Joe's was located on campus in University Square, about a ten-minute walk from my apartment. The place looked like what you'd expect from a college hangout, with low ceilings, wood paneling and framed photographs on the wall. It was noisy and crowded with students. There was a jukebox playing '80s music. Candace looked around until a red-haired woman waved to us from across the room. Candace took my arm. "We're over there."

We pushed our way through the restaurant to the east corner, where a group of five students were sitting at a table with a half-eaten pizza and two large pitchers of beer. The man at the head of the table looked a little like James Dean. His hair was golden brown and he wore a cotton oxford shirt unbuttoned to his chest, with the sleeves rolled up. He looked at me coolly.

"Everyone, this is Luke," Candace said.

Everyone waved or bobbed their heads except for the James Dean look-alike who studied me for a moment before speaking. "Luke-warm," he said. "I'm Sean. Have a beer."

"Thanks," I said.

Candace and I sat down. Candace said, "That's Marshall, Suzie, Lucy and James."

"Hi," I said.

A tall blond guy reached across the table and shook my hand. "I'm Marshall."

"Hi," I said.

"What's your last name, Luke?" Sean asked.

"Crisp."

"Crisp, like, Crisp's Copy Centers?" asked James, a thin, olive-skinned man with dark brown curly hair.

"Yeah, just like it," I said, purposely not making the connection.

"That's not a common name," Lucy said. Lucy was the woman who had waved to us as we entered. She was a resplendent redhead with beautiful emerald green eyes, full lips and a shapely figure. She had one hand on Marshall's arm, so I assumed they were together. "Are you any relation to the owners of Crisp's?"

"It's my father's company," I said.

Candace looked at me in surprise.

"Carl Crisp is your father?" Marshall practically shouted. "I read his *Forbes* write-up last April. Now there's a capitalist. He's put more people out of business than Hurricane Katrina."

"Who's your father," I asked sharply, "Che Guevara?"

Everyone laughed except Marshall.

"Che Guevara. That's good," Sean said, looking impressed. "Then you're definitely one of us. We are the fruit of capitalism and the spawn of privilege. We have everything and we have nothing." He raised a beer. "To champagne dreams and cardboard souls."

The phrase made me smile. I wondered how closely it truly described him.

"Cardboard souls," echoed Suzie, a very thin young woman with short blond hair.

"So, Mr. Crisp," Sean said, his gaze settling on me. "What is the meaning of life?"

Candace rolled her eyes.

"He asks everyone that," Lucy said.

I felt a little awkward. "Haven't answered that one yet, Sean. I'm just happy to be here."

"I like that," Candace said.

"Yes, the unexamined life," Sean said, "That is a statement of its own. Now James, here, says he's a born-again, whatever that means . . ."

"It means I'm Christian," he said to me.

"As I said, whatever that means," Sean said. "Making fun of Christians is like hunting cows with a machine gun."

James just shook his head.

"Now Lucy here is an agnostic, even though that's kind of a big word for her . . ."

Lucy playfully hit him.

". . . And Marshall is a hedonist."

"*Altruistic* hedonist," Marshall corrected.

"What is an altruistic hedonist?" I asked.

Marshall said, "We believe that the only things in life worth pursuing are beauty and pleasure—the honest fulfillment of the senses. But, we also acknowledge that altruism brings a type of pleasure as well."

"I haven't figured out what Suzie is," Sean said.

"Moral capitalist," Suzie said.

"There's an oxymoron for you," Marshall said.

"What am I?" Candace asked.

"You," Sean replied slowly, "are careful."

Candace shrugged. "Unlike you," she said.

"So what are you?" I asked Sean.

He smiled. "I am deeply superficial."

"Which means he doesn't know what he is," Suzie said.

"Which means," Sean said, "that I'm not arrogant enough to claim that I know the meaning of life, if there is such a thing."

"Did you actually use the words 'not' and 'arrogant' to describe yourself?" Candace asked.

"Since you all have handles," I said, "I suppose I'm a capitalist too. That's why we're chasing the M.B.A. carrot, right?"

"I love carrots," Lucy said. She turned to me. "I'm vegan."

Marshall said, "Now hold on, that doesn't preclude you from being a hedonist. Would you say your capitalism is a means or an end?"

"A means or an end to what?" I asked.

"Let me put it this way," Marshall said, "If you had a billion dollars, would you keep on working?"

I thought about it. "Probably."

"Then you're as much a hedonist as me."

"How did you come to that conclusion?" Candace asked.

"I'm just saying, that if your ultimate goal is to make

money for the sake of making money, then you are the most extreme of hedonists, taking pleasure in the most obscure of pleasures."

"Marshall's right," Sean said. "Modern capitalism has created a new aesthetic, a shiny new species of man—one who doesn't value what money can buy, only money itself. It's like preparing a feast just to look at it."

"That can be pleasurable too," Candace said.

"You," Sean said, pointing at Candace, "don't talk so much."

Candace rolled her eyes.

"There's always been that man," I said. "Just read Dickens."

"You're right," Sean said, nodding, "Our culture has invented nothing, it just unabashedly embraces cultures' past failures—wipes them off and calls them new. It's philosophically fascinating—the relativists have asserted for centuries that the journey *is* the destination, and this new breed of capitalist is living that. Create and hoard. It's poetic."

"I don't know why anyone would bother," Lucy said, "It's too much work. I say, work to live, not live to work. Just enough to afford life's pleasures."

"What do you know about work?" Marshall asked.

"Ask me what I know about pleasure," she replied, leaning into him.

"Well, it does raise interesting questions," Candace said, "How much is enough? Are we born for greed or good? And, ultimately, what is good?"

"*That's* the right question," Sean said, touching the tip of his nose as if we were playing charades. "Greed *is* good."

"*God* is good," James said. He had spoken so little I'd almost forgotten he was there.

"This might surprise you," Sean said, turning to James, "but for once I'm not disagreeing with you, my twice-born friend. If you believe in God and that God is good, then it would be wrong to not acknowledge the good He's created. It would be like worshiping the tree but shunning its fruit. Good is to be found in the pursuit of the pleasures of the world."

"So today you're a hedonist," Marshall said.

"Hedonist *and* believer. Think about it. If you believe in the one All Mighty Creator, then look at what He's created: the sensual pleasures, food, drink, flesh—they're His creations, not ours—created for our enjoyment. And that is the only God worth worshiping, the one who created us . . ."

"Or *we* created," interjected Marshall.

". . . Or we created," Sean agreed. "The God who wants us to experience true pleasure. Anything less is masochism. And that's Lucy's deal, not mine."

Lucy grinned.

"She'd have to be a masochist to stay with Marshall," Suzie said.

Sean raised a glass. "To greed, hedonism and the One True God who gave it to the world."

Candace was right. Her friends were anything but dull.

CHAPTER

Six

What a difference having a friend makes . . .

 Luke Crisp's Diary

Candace and I left Smokey Joe's a few hours later. It was dark outside and the temperature had fallen, necessitating a brisker pace. "So what did you think of my friends?" Candace asked.

"Interesting."

"Interesting *good* or interesting *bad*?"

"Keeping up with their banter is the mental equivalent of a treadmill," I said.

She burst out laughing, which had a sweet, joyful ring to it. "Exactly. Sometimes when you're with them you just want to drink yourself stupid. I never take them too seriously, but every now and then they'll say something worth thinking about."

"So I take it that Sean's the leader?"

"Pretty much."

"Tell me about him."

"Sean's the son of a very wealthy Boston investment banker. He's worldly, you know? He's like a collegiate sha-man. He's got this amazing sense—he knows every party and can get into any of them. He's likable, don't you think?"

I nodded. "He's very charismatic."

"Yeah, he is. I could tell he liked you."

"How could you tell?"

"Believe me, you'd know if he didn't." She brushed her hair back from her face. "Lucy and Suzie both have a thing for him."

"I thought Lucy was with Marshall."

"She is. But I'm pretty sure that's by default. The girls all want Sean."

"You too?"

"Present company excluded," she said. "Sean's not exactly the kind of foundation you'd want to build on, if you know what I mean."

"Are they all in Wharton?"

"No. Lucy's working on her undergrad at UPenn. Same with Suzie. I think she's an art major. Sean and Marshall met them at a club."

"What's James's story? He didn't really seem to fit in with Sean and Marshall."

"No, I'm not sure why he hangs out with them," she said. "James comes from a military family, so there's no money. He's at Wharton on a scholarship and he works on the side. He owns an office-cleaning business."

"He seems more serious than the others."

"He is. He misses a lot of our get-togethers to actually study. He's also the only one of the group who goes to church, which Sean enjoys mocking."

"Then why does he hang out with them?"

"Like I said, I'm not sure why. Maybe he thinks he can save their souls."

"It doesn't seem to be working," I said.

"No, I don't think so."

"How about you?" I asked. "Are you religious?"

"Not really. I go to church now and then, Christmas, Easter, that kind of thing. And you?"

"I did when I was little. When my mother was still alive."

"You lost your mother?"

"When I was seven."

She looked at me sympathetically. "I'm sorry. That must have been horrible."

"It was." I turned to her. "So, how did you answer Sean's question? What is the meaning of life?"

"I think," she said deliberately, "the meaning of life is exactly what one says it is."

✦

We arrived at our apartment building and walked in. We stopped in front of the elevator.

"Tell me something," I said. "Why did you invite me tonight?"

She smiled. "I don't know. I've just noticed you in class. Something about you intrigued me." She added, "There's more to you."

"More?"

"I don't know how to explain it. Solidness."

I grinned a little. "Solidness, huh? You're saying I'm thick?"

"No, I'm saying you have substance. I've lived with enough hollow people to know."

"I'll take that as a compliment," I said.

"I meant it as one," she replied. "So, my turn. Why did you accept my invitation?"

"Unfortunately, my answer will completely refute all you just said."

"Yes?"

"I thought you had beautiful eyes."

A broad smile crossed her face. A moment later the elevator door opened and we both stepped inside. I pushed the button for my floor and hers. When we reached the third floor, she leaned forward and pecked me on the cheek. "Thanks again for coming. I'll see you in class." She stepped out of the elevator and turned back. "Good night, Luke."

"Good night, Candace."

She waved goodbye as the doors closed. Wharton was already looking a whole lot better.

CHAPTER

Seven

The law of centrifugal force seems to be as true for the human condition as it is for Newtonian mechanics— the faster our lives spin, the more things tend to fly apart.

✦ Luke Crisp's Diary ✦

After that first evening, Candace and I started seeing each other three or four times a week. She fascinated me. She was smart, though more streetwise than academically. She confided in me that she struggled in most of her classes.

Candace asked a lot of questions about my childhood but didn't offer much about her own. I never had the sense that she was hiding anything as much as she just didn't care to talk about it. All I really knew about her past was that she had moved a lot, and her parents had divorced a year before she started college, something that had profoundly affected her. As I got to know her better, I began to understand her comment about being attracted to my "solidness." She seemed afraid of the unknown—especially in financial matters. What Sean had called her, "careful," was right on. Both confident *and* careful, if that's possible. I had never met anyone quite like her.

Looking back, my feelings for Candace crept up on me with such stealth that I couldn't tell you when I actually fell in love, but it was in early November that I knew I was hooked. I suppose I had never really been in love before— I'm not saying there hadn't been women in my life, or, at least, girls; there had and I'd had crushes on more than a few of them—but my feelings for Candace were something new. Something powerful. And they were growing stronger. I found myself spending every free moment I could with her and thinking about her when I wasn't with her. It may have had something to do with growing up without a mother, but I became enamored with her maternal nature. Once I got a paper cut and she immediately grabbed my hand and kissed my finger. I loved it. I loved her.

I've heard it said that more than a few men have been dashed to bits on the reef of femininity. If I wasn't sunk, I was, at least, run aground. Within six weeks of our meeting we decided to only see each other.

The "study group" continued to meet weekly, and Sean and I became friends as well. The relationship was refreshing. Outside of my father, I hadn't had a close male friend in years.

·✦·

My school career rose and fell with the usual tides of academia, and I just floated through it, lost in love. As I became enmeshed in my new world, my previous life seemed to drift further and further away. My father and I emailed or texted almost every day, though usually it was just a quick note, "How are things? How's business? How's school?" He'd occasionally allude to some of the copy centers' happenings, but not as much as I thought he would—always sharing more information about the people than the profits. I shouldn't have been surprised. He had sent me away to find life out-side of Crisp's and he wasn't about to sabotage his own plans.

✦

Crisp's went public in late November with 100 million shares. Henry kept me abreast of the offering, texting me four or five times throughout the day. The stock was issued at a dollar a share and rose to $3.42 by the time the market closed. The Wharton 7 knew about it before I told them. They were congregated in the usual corner of Smokey Joe's when Candace and I arrived.

"So your old man's worth a few hundred mill," Marshall said as we approached the table. Candace and I sat down.

"Apparently," I said.

"That's a lot of calzone," Sean said. "Congratulations."

"So," Marshall said, leaning toward me. "What's your share of the booty?"

"What makes you think I have a share?"

"Do you have any siblings?" Lucy asked.

"No."

"Holy cannoli," Marshall said, "It's all yours someday. I think I'll start being nicer to you."

Suzie said, "How do you even get motivated to study when you've got a parachute like that?"

"I wouldn't mind finding out," Marshall said. "If you're lucky, the old man will croak soon."

I felt my face turn red and I spun at him. "Why don't you just shut up?"

Marshall looked at me blankly, caught in the stupidity of his comment. "Sorry, I didn't mean . . ."

"You're an idiot," Sean said. "It's his father." Sean turned to me. "Sorry, man. Don't listen to him."

Marshall turned pale. "I wasn't serious."

I stood. "Let's go," I said to Candace.

"Luke," Marshall said, "it was a stupid joke."

"You're a stupid joke," Candace said.

We walked out of the pub. James followed us out. "Hey, Luke. Sorry about that. You know how Marshall is. I'm sure he didn't mean it."

"Of course he did," Candace said. "And why are you making excuses for Marshall? He and Sean mock you every time you open your mouth."

"They're just joking around," he said. James looked truly worried about my feelings.

"It's not a big deal," I finally said. "I just need to cool off."

He looked relieved. "All right," he said, patting my shoulder. "And congratulations. Success couldn't happen to a nicer guy."

After he went back into the pub, Candace said, "Of all of them to be happy for your father's success, you wouldn't expect it to be James. He has the most to envy."

"He's a good guy," I said. "He reminds me of my father. You watch, he'll go further than any of us."

CHAPTER

Eight

*As a boy, I fantasized a "Currier and Ives" Christmas,
dragging home a pine tree through pristine banks of crystalline snow.
Unfortunately, in Phoenix, we'd be more likely
to find a cactus than a pine.
No matter. Like Heaven, Christmas is less about the weather
than the company.*

✦ Luke Crisp's Diary ✦

That December I went home for Christmas. It was my first time back since I had left for school. I asked Candace to come with me, but she had commitments with her own family. It was her year to spend Christmas with her father, who would otherwise spend the holiday alone.

"I couldn't do that to him," she said, "Besides, it's still a little early to start meeting parents." She must have seen the disappointment on my face when she said that, because she kissed me on the cheek, then added, "But not by much."

＊

It was good to go home again. The mild Arizona winter was a stark, welcome contrast to the flesh-numbing cold of Philly. My father had invited his only brother, Paul, and his wife, Barbara, over for Christmas Eve dinner, which had been the routine for the past six Christmases, ever since the last of their children had married off and moved out of state. My father also invited his assistant, Mary, who was as close as family.

As usual, my father had our dinner catered with the exception of the turkey and stuffing, which was his own specialty. We sat down to eat at the long table in the dining room that was used more often for business meetings than eating.

After we'd settled in, Barbara asked me, "So how is school going?"

"It's good," I said.

"Luke's been doing well," my father said.

"How are things on the romantic front?" Barbara asked, which was probably what she had meant by her first question.

"I have a girlfriend," I said.

"Oh. Does she have a name?"

"Candace."

"Candace. That's a pretty name."

"Where's she from?" Paul asked.

"Cincinnati."

"Do you have any plans?" Barbara asked.

I said without looking up, "I've got lots of plans."

"You know what I mean."

I grinned. "No. Not yet."

"But you've discussed marriage."

"We've talked," I said.

My father looked at me with surprise.

"Wonderful," Barbara said, "Just wonderful. Let us know when something happens."

"You'll be among the first to know," I said.

My father still said nothing, but I sensed that he was pleased.

·✦·

After dinner, we ate pecan pie, then talked over coffee until dark. After everyone had left, my father put his hand on my shoulder. "I want to show you something."

"How are things going with the business?" I asked, following him out of the room.

"Okay," he said in a tone that suggested otherwise. "We're still growing in this economy," he said. "The shareholders are happy."

"You don't sound very happy," I said.

"I'm not sure I was ready to go public. It's one thing to run a family business, it's a whole different beast to have shareholders to answer to."

We walked into his den. "But you still own the majority of stock," I said. "You can do as you please."

He grinned. "It's not that simple. There's such a thing as fiduciary responsibility. Stockholders have rights."

"Then you regret going public?"

"Sometimes. But I can't dismiss the good. The capital infusion has allowed us to exponentially increase our growth. Besides," he said, looking into my eyes, "I won't be here to run things forever."

"Sure you will," I said. "You're immortal."

He smiled. Then he pulled something down from a shelf—a leather binder embossed with his initials, CC, overlapped as they might be on a branding iron. He handed it to me. "Here you go."

"What is it?" I asked.

"Like I said, I won't be here to run things forever. These are my detailed instructions in the event that something happens to me. I've made you the executor of my estate."

I looked at him anxiously. "Why are you giving this to me now?"

He read the concern on my face and casually waved it off. "It's nothing. You know me, measure twice and cut once. It's better to err on the side of caution. We Crisps aren't exactly known for longevity. I'm already two years older than my father was when he passed away and six years older than my grandfather was."

"I don't like talking about this," I said.

"I know. And I'm just . . ." His expression lightened. "It's like the flight attendants' announcement, 'In the unlikely event of a water landing . . .' I've prepared all the documents on what I'd like done with my assets: life insurance policies, personal property, charities, etcetera, etcetera. Also, what I'd like to see happen to our top managers." My father was always watching over those in the business. "Also, you should know that you have a trust fund that you are already of age to access."

"I have plenty," I said. "You already pay for everything."

"I know, it's just legal hogwash. But the trust fund is completely in your name so you need to be aware of it." He knew I wouldn't ask, so he offered. "There's a million dollars in it."

I handed him back the binder. "How about we just agree that nothing ever happens to you."

He smiled. "Agreed. Want to play some chess?"

"Bring it on," I said. "You're going down, old man."

"After all that money I've spent on your education, I certainly hope so."

I had almost forgotten how much I enjoyed being with my father.

CHAPTER

Everything human is evolving. Always.
That includes our hearts and desires as well as our bodies.

✦ Luke Crisp's Diary ✦

Christmas was gone in a blink and I was back in the cold of Philly. No matter what they say, distance *doesn't* make the heart grow fonder—it makes it *cooler*, like an ember pulled from a fire. I could say that I had never experienced this phenomenon, but that wouldn't really be true. My mother's absence was all I thought about as a boy—now it rarely even crossed my mind.

As I became fully engrossed in my new world and my father became overwhelmed by the requisite business of running a public corporation, our relationship changed. *Cooled,* you might say. It happened so gradually I don't think I was even aware of it.

I say that my father was "running" the company, but in actuality it was more like being dragged behind it. In the few emails from him that mentioned Crisp's, his comments seemed more about obligation than passion—and my father had always been passionate about business. "Without passion, we are destined to mediocrity," he taught. Truthfully, I was becoming less passionate about someday running Crisp's as well.

As my relationship with my father weakened, my relationship with Candace grew stronger. So did my friendship with Sean. When I wasn't with Candace, I was usually with him. I suppose that both provided something I was looking for. Sean was a man who knew how to live. He worked as hard at playing as most people did at their careers. At the end of our spring semester he organized a trip to St. Barts in the French West Indies. I didn't know anything about St. Barts, but Sean did and he painted a picture of the island better than any travel agent could—brilliant white sand beaches against an equally brilliant blue sea—upscale boutiques and an abundance of the finest French food and women this side of the Atlantic.

Sean invited the Wharton 7 to join him. Marshall and Lucy were in, but Suzie had other plans and James didn't have the money to go. Neither did Candace, but I didn't want to go without her, so I offered to pay her way. She felt embarrassed about me footing her bill and resisted until I talked her into it.

The morning of our departure, the five of us gathered at Sean's place—Chez Sean, he called it: a small home he had rented about a mile from the campus. We were about to leave for the airport when the doorbell rang.

"Somebody get that," Sean said.

"Got it," I said. I answered the door to find my father standing on the front porch.

For a moment I just looked at him in surprise. "Dad. What are you doing here?"

He smiled. "I had a meeting in Philly and thought I'd drop by and surprise you."

"Wow. Yeah, you did. How did you know I was here?"

"Luck. When I went to your room, one of the students told me you were here."

In light of our impending departure I wasn't sure what to say. After a moment he said, "May I come in?"

"Sorry. Of course. Actually, we were just getting ready to go to the airport. We're flying to St. Barts."

"St. Barts. Oh. Sorry, I didn't know."

"I should have told you. It was kind of last-minute."

He looked a little awkward. "Well, then maybe I should just go."

"No. We have a little time. Come in. Let me introduce you to everyone."

I led my father into the kitchen area, where our luggage and everyone but Sean was gathered. Candace and Marshall immediately stood.

"Candace, this is my father."

She walked up to him. "I'm Candace," she said, smiling sweetly.

"My pleasure, Candace. Luke's told me a lot about you."

"He's told me a lot about you too," she said. "I'm really happy to finally meet you."

I pointed to the others. "And that's Marshall and Lucy."

My father waved. "Hello."

Lucy waved back. Marshall walked up to my father. "It's an honor to meet you, sir. I've read at least a half dozen articles about you."

"Don't believe everything you read," my father said lightly.

Just then Sean walked into the room holding a beer. "Who was it?" When he saw my father, he set his beer down on the counter. "Mr. Crisp," he said. "Welcome."

"This is Sean," I said. "This is his place."

I've heard it said that some people have the *gift of discernment*—the ability to see through a person's guises and pretenses right to their very soul. If anyone had that gift, it was my father. I once attended a business meeting between him and a potential investor. Just fifteen minutes into the meeting my father thanked the man for his time but told him that he wasn't interested. After we were alone, I asked my father what was wrong with the deal. "Nothing," he said. "I don't trust the dealer." Two years later I read an article about that same businessman in our local newspaper. He had just been convicted of fraud.

Knowing this, my father's reaction to Sean should have meant something to me. My father's brow furrowed and he tensed a little, the way he did when he was skeptical of what he was hearing. Still, my father was always polite. He put out his hand. "Nice to meet you, Sean."

"Likewise," Sean said. "It's an honor." I think it was the first time I had ever seen Sean look nervous.

My father turned back to me. "Well, I'll get out of your way so you can go."

"All right," I said. I walked my father to the door. Everything about the situation was awkward. On the porch he turned back to me. "Are you well?"

"I'm fine," I said. "I'm sorry about this. If I had known . . ."

"No, it's my fault. I should have called first."

"Well, thanks for coming by."

"Be safe," he said.

"Okay. Good luck with your meeting."

He looked at me as if he were about to say something, then instead he turned away and walked to his car. I waved to him as he drove away. Then I went back inside to get my luggage. We had a plane to catch.

CHAPTER

Ten

Someone should invent a pill for guilt.
They'd make billions.

 Luke Crisp's Diary

In June the Wharton 7 fell to 6 when Suzie dropped out of school to work for her father's trucking company. Around that same time I gave in to Sean's repeated request to move off campus into Chez Sean. Candace was against the idea from the beginning.

"You're really going to room with Sean?" she asked.

"I take it you disapprove."

"Sean's like radiation—okay only in small doses."

"You're afraid I'll start losing my hair?"

"Your hair I can handle. It's your soul I worry about."

"My soul," I laughed.

"You hang around Sean long enough and he's bound to rub off on you."

"You're making too much of this," I said. "What's the worst thing that could happen?"

She folded her arms. "You could become like Sean."

"It's only a year," I said. "How much could I change in a year?"

"I don't want to find out," she replied.

In spite of Candace's disapproval, two weeks later I moved into Chez Sean. Living with Sean was a window to a whole new paradigm. Sean was naturally intelligent, maybe even a genius, but fundamentally lazy—a dangerous combination. He got good grades without ever studying. He was not ashamed of being lazy, rather, he wore it as a badge of honor, proclaiming himself ethically superior to the "poor working saps who sold their heartbeats to the devil of the marketplace." On his refrigerator door was a sign which read,

> *Life was meant to be lived—*
> *not feared, sold, nor sweated.*
> *Fear not death. Fear the unlived life.*

The night I moved in, he raised a toast. "Let the masses cling to their sorry lives of quiet desperation. Let them rust in obscurity—we, my friend, shall be found among the living."

Over the next year I learned what he meant by "living."

✦

When I was twelve years old, my father told me a story about boiling a frog. "If you throw a frog into boiling water," he said, "It will jump out. But if you put the frog in a pot of warm water and slowly turn up the heat, it won't notice the change and the frog will eventually boil to death."

I think that Sean understood this principle instinctively. He was the flame and I was his frog. The changes in my life came gradually, beginning with an occasional, casual invitation to a party here and there. Looking back, I'm certain that Sean purposely didn't invite me to the wilder ones, knowing I would be uncomfortable and might avoid his future invitations. But it seemed that each party I went to got a little wilder. So did I.

Sean, as a matter of personal philosophy, tried everything that came his way and, in the lofty name of freedom, urged me to do likewise. Most of the time I didn't. Most of the time I ignored his temptations. Most of the time. But not always.

My first fail was drinking too much. Both my father and I drank, occasionally, but never to excess. That changed. Sean drank a lot at home and I eventually began joining him. Only a little at first, then more and more. Everyone drank heavily at parties he took me to and soon I did too. For the first time in my life, I woke in a strange house with no idea of how I had got there.

One boring Tuesday night Sean and I got hammered in Chez Sean. There was no reason in particular—we just didn't stop drinking. I had a class the next morning with Candace, and I walked in late with my head throbbing, desperately wishing that someone would dim the lights.

As I sat down, Candace said, "You smell like a liquor cabinet."

"I took a shower," I said.

"It's like coming from your skin. You're stinking up the room."

I looked around me. A few other students were looking at

me. I looked back at her and shrugged. "What's the big deal? I just had too much to drink last night."

"Why were you drinking on a random Tuesday?"

"Sean and I . . ."

"Sean," she said as if she needed no further explanation. She didn't talk to me for the rest of the class.

✦

Late that evening my father called me for the first time in months.

"How are you?" he asked. His voice was tight. Serious.

"I'm fine," I answered tentatively. "How are you?"

"How are you handling the pressure of school?"

His tone worried me. "I'm doing fine," I repeated. "Why?"

"I just got a call from Chuck. He said you were drunk in class this morning." Chuck was my father's friend, the one who had helped expedite my admission into Wharton.

"I wasn't drunk."

"Why would Chuck tell me that?"

"You have your friend spying on me?"

"Of course not. He heard it from your professor."

"I told you, I wasn't drunk."

"He said the classroom smelled like booze."

"That part may be true," I said. "But I wasn't drunk. I just had a lot to drink the night before."

"What's going on, Luke?"

"Nothing's going on. I just drank too much. It's not like you don't drink."

"I don't walk into board meetings stinking of booze. How often are you drinking?"

"Why are you interrogating me?" I snapped. "I'm old enough to be making my own decisions without you checking up on me."

My response seemed to stun him. He was silent for a moment then said, "You're right. I just care about you."

I took a deep breath. "I'm sorry," I said. "But I'm fine." More silence. Finally I said, "I need to go."

"I love you, Luke."

"All right," I said and hung up.

Things had changed between us even more than I realized. Or maybe I had changed more than I realized. I had never talked to my father like that before. I set down my phone, then dropped my head into my hands.

Sean had overheard my conversation and walked into the room carrying a can of beer. "Who was that?"

"My father. Someone at Wharton called him and told him I was drunk in class this morning."

"You weren't drunk," he said. "A little hungover, but not drunk."

"I shouted at my dad."

Sean grinned. "Welcome to my world."

I didn't like the sound of that. "It's not my world."

"It happens," he said.

"Not to me," I said. "Do you even have any contact with your parents?"

"My mother," he said. "She's the one who keeps me in the green. My father disowned me."

"What happened?"

"Same old story. He was never around when I was growing up. When he was, we fought. A few years ago, on Christmas Eve, we had a big fight in front of like fifty of his guests. I called him a vulture capitalist. He responded by telling me what a disappointment I was to him as a son.

"I said, 'You don't think being your son is a disappointment?' He said 'Fine. Have it your way. I wash my hands of you.' "

I honestly couldn't think of anything worse. "What did you say to that?"

He looked at me with dark eyes. "I thanked him."

"You thanked him?"

"I meant it. It was liberating. I was tired of him orchestrating my life, telling me what I was going to do and be. I was tired of the strings that came with his money. I hadn't sold my soul to the devil, I had leased it."

"How did your mother respond?"

"My mother was his first trophy wife. By then he was on to trophy wife number two, so she shares my enmity." He took a drink from his beer. "What about you? Daddy's got it all figured out for you too? Got the master plan?"

"My father's not making me do anything," I said.

"But he's kept you close to the business, hasn't he? Groomed you to be the heir? The next *him*."

I didn't answer.

"I thought so," Sean said. "I'm not saying he's my father. I'm just saying it's the natural law—fathers creating their sons in their own image. It's a Judeo-Christian archetype. You see it in the cathedral, as well as on the Little League baseball diamond. You see it every day at Wharton." He hit me on the shoulder. "So when you finish here, is that the next act? Going home to mind the family store?"

"That's what my father wants." I felt infantile saying that.

"What do *you* want?"

I slowly shook my head. "I'm not sure anymore."

Sean leaned close. "That's a dangerous place to be, my friend. The undecided get swept away by the momentum of the decided. I can see it now, you'll graduate from Wharton, then go back to the desert, settle down with the little woman, plant a garden in the graveyard out back and watch yourself grow fat and arthritic on a domestic death march."

"That's how it goes?" I said, annoyed by his cynicism.

"Far as I can see. People don't really live longer these days, they just die slower. We've traded the American dream for a charge card at the local Home Depot. What a crock."

"What are your plans when you graduate?"

"My plans," he said. "Marshall, Lucy and I are going to get drunk in seven countries."

"Why seven?"

"It's my lucky number," he said. "I figure by that point I'll have vomited up all the crap they've forced down my throat the last eighteen years of American capitalist indoctrination. Then I'm going to just get drunk for the sheer debauchery of it." He looked at me. "You should come with us. You've got plenty of time to die the slow death."

"You're dismal tonight."

"Come with us."

"I have Candace."

"Bring her. Show her life before she gives birth to creatures she loves more than you and you're relegated to the status of beast of burden."

"You are past dismal."

"You know I'm telling the truth. Give life a chance."

"You sound like an infomercial for Hedonists International," I said. "Eat, drink and be merry for tomorrow we may die."

"There's no 'may' about it. Tomorrow we *will* die." He pointed at me with the hand holding his can. "The only real sin that exists in this life is the waste of possibility. The rest of our sins are just part of the learning curve. God, if there is such a thing, rejoices in our passion. It's the lukewarm He spits from His mouth. You can read it in the Bible." Sean leaned in close. "I know you, Luke. You're special. Marshall and Lucy may talk like freethinkers, but they're not. In the end, you'll find them washed up on the beach of circumstance with the rest of the conformists. But you, my friend, have the potential of doing something spectacular with your allotted time—to be a beacon of hope to the yoked, desperate masses, a light on the hill of possibility. You owe it to the world."

I laughed at his flattery. "I have nothing to offer the world."

Sean's expression turned serious. "Don't ever let anyone tell you that. Don't sell your soul to the devils of obscurity. What about *your* dreams? Do you even know what they are anymore?"

I didn't answer, which I suppose was an answer in itself.

He slowly shook his head. "The world is yours, Luke. At least check it out before you throw it away."

I stood. "I'm going to bed," I said.

Sean just stared at me. "Think about coming with us. Just think about it."

CHAPTER

Eleven

As a species we care less about the truth than our agendas.
We really don't want to know the truth. We must not.
Why else would we work so hard to hide from it?

✦ Luke Crisp's Diary ✦

Drinking wasn't my only new vice. Sean was a self-proclaimed "chick magnet," which, from my observation, seemed to be true. For whatever reason, women flocked to him and he was always willing to share from his excess. At first I refused his offers, citing my loyalty to Candace, which Sean found naïve. "You're not married. You're not even engaged," he said, later adding, "The man who doesn't sow his oats when he's young, will do so when he's old."

If you pound at anything long enough, it's bound to fracture. One evening, about six months after moving in with Sean, I broke. Candace was busy that night, so I went with Sean to a UPenn party he'd found out about. I drank too much and ended up spending the night with a coed whose name I didn't even know. The next morning I woke filled with burning shame. When I told Sean that I was going to confess to Candace, he erupted. "Don't be stupid. What good could possibly come of that?"

"She would want to know the truth," I said.

"Is that really why? Or are you just trying to shift your pain to her?"

"What are you talking about?" I said.

"All you'll do is turn *your* guilt into *her* broken heart and ruin the best thing you've got going. You were drunk. If you're not willing to give yourself a break, then at least give her one."

I never told Candace, though I think she suspected something. That evening at dinner she looked at me with a peculiar expression, as if something were different but she couldn't put her finger on it. "You're not yourself tonight."

"It's nothing," I said forcefully enough to convince her otherwise. "I just have a headache."

"Do you need an Advil?"

"I'm okay," I said.

"I called you last night. You never answered."

I poked at my dinner, avoiding her gaze. "I was out with Sean," I said. "We were drinking."

"I called you this morning too. Where were you?"

"I told you, we were drinking. I was just sleeping it off."

I must have looked guilty, because she looked at me for a minute, then she asked, "Is there anything else you want to tell me?"

Anger at her question rose within me. I snapped at her, "Enough with the interrogation, already!"

She flinched. "I'm sorry. I just wish you'd stop drinking so much."

"I know," I said.

"Sean's not good for you."

"I know," I said again.

We went back to our meal as if nothing had happened.

CHAPTER

Twelve

Guilt makes strangers of us all.

✦ Luke Crisp's Diary ✦

As graduation neared, I was filled with a myriad of emotions, all of which seemed to contribute to the chasm that had developed between my father and me.

Of course time and distance played their part in our rift, but the biggest reason took a much wiser and older me to understand. Perhaps it's an archetype, like Adam hiding from God after partaking of the fruit, but on some level I believe that I was hiding from my father because of whom I had become. In spite of my outward denials, to myself as well as to others, I carried an enormous amount of guilt for my choices—and guilt always estranges us. The truth was, I was afraid of my father's rejection, so I rejected him first.

✦

A month before graduation Mary, my father's assistant, called me.

"Luke, it's Mary. Your father wanted me to call about your graduation. We need to make his travel arrangements."

I hesitated. "Don't worry about it."

"Don't worry about what?"

"Attending the graduation ceremony. It's not important. I'll be home a few days after anyway."

Mary sounded vexed. "It's important to your father. He's very proud of you."

"Tell him that I appreciate the sentiment, but if it's all the same, I'd rather not make a big deal over it."

She was quiet for a moment, then said, "All right. I'll tell him."

I don't know if I'd hurt my father's feelings or if he was just respecting my wishes, but my father never called to talk me out of it.

✦

A few hours after our graduation ceremony the Wharton 6 gathered for a final session at Smokey Joe's.

"So what's going down tonight?" Marshall asked, nursing a tall beer. Lucy stood behind him, her arms wrapped around him.

"There's a party on Delancey Street," Sean said. "A night of pure debauchery." He turned to James. "You'll want to sit this one out."

"Thanks for the warning," James said.

Actually, I was kind of surprised to see James, as he hadn't been around for a while.

"What do you think?" I asked Candace. "Want to go?"

She frowned. "Remember, my mother's in town."

"Oh yeah," I said. I had no interest in spending graduation night hanging out with Candace's mother. Neither did Candace for that matter.

Marshall said, "Hang with us, Luke. Let's go out with a bang."

"Yes, Luke, give in to the dark side," Sean said. "I am your father, Luke."

"C'mon," Lucy said. "It will be fun."

I looked at Candace for permission. She said, "Do what you want."

"All right," I said to Sean. "I'm in."

"Great," he said.

"Awesome," Marshall said. "The final stand of the Wharton 6 minus James. And Candace. And, whoever else doesn't show up."

⋆

As we were all leaving Smokey Joe's, James grabbed my shoulder. "Hey, are you really going to that party?"

"Yeah. Why don't you join us?"

"No, I'm not into that junk."

"What junk?"

"People throwing up. Brawling. Waking up in strange places with stranger people. I thought I'd get some people together—grill some steaks, watch 24."

"Sounds like you've got a plan," I said.

"Why don't you come?" he asked. "It will be fun."

"Sorry, I already committed."

"I'm upping the ante," James said. "I'll make my sautéed

mushrooms in burgundy wine sauce. Can't beat my burgundy 'shrooms."

"Sorry, James."

"I really can't talk you into it?"

"No. Let's get pancakes in the morning. We'll go to IHOP, my treat."

He looked dejected. "In the morning? Think you'll be up for it?"

"Just not too early," I said.

He forced a smile. "Okay, man. But if you change your mind, call me."

"I will. Thanks."

As I watched him walk away, something told me to go with him. I almost did. I should have. Both of our lives would have been different if I had.

CHAPTER

Thirteen

*They say that life is what happens to you
when you're making other plans.*

So is death.

✦ Luke Crisp's Diary ✦

For once, the party wasn't all Sean claimed it would be. As usual, he was drunk by eleven and left the party with some young blonde who looked like she was barely eighteen. Lucy and Marshall left a half hour later. I stayed and drank and listened to some woman tell me why she'd dumped her boyfriend—an agonizingly long prelude to informing me that she was available and desperate. I wished I had gone with James. I wished I had gone with Candace for that matter. It was a wasted night.

✦

I woke the next morning to Candace shaking me. "Luke, wake up."

I rolled over in bed and opened my eyes. The morning light glared through my window and my head throbbed from too many beers. Then I realized that Sean, Marshall, Lucy and Candace were all standing above me.

"What are you doing here?" I asked.

"Did you hear about James?" Candace asked.

"James? We're supposed to get pancakes this morning."

Candace looked over at Marshall. The look on their faces troubled me.

"What are you doing here?" I repeated. "What's going on?"

Sean looked at me with dull eyes. "James was in an accident."

I looked back and forth between them. "What?"

"Last night," Marshall said, "He was hit by a drunk driver."

Sleep left me. "Is he okay? Where is he?"

"He was killed," Candace said.

I sat up. "Killed? I just . . . I was just with him. We're going to get pancakes." I looked back and forth between them. "This can't be."

"It's true," Candace said.

I felt sick to my stomach. "No, it can't be." My eyes began to well up with tears.

Candace sat down on the bed next to me. "I'm sorry, baby."

"If I had gone with him . . ." I said.

"If you had gone with him, you might have been killed too," Marshall said. "He was hit by some drunk kid celebrating his graduation. The kid ran a red light and hit James in a crosswalk."

"I just can't believe it," I said. "Why James? He did everything by the book. He worked hard, he went to church, he believed in God. None of it saved him."

"The good die young," Sean said.

"It's not right," Candace said.

"It's not a matter of right or wrong," Sean said, "it's what is and what isn't. Death can come at any time. Accept it or not, death comes all the same. The only question is, what are you going to do about it."

✦

Three days after graduation we attended James's funeral in Philadelphia. He was buried with his graduation sash, the family's first college graduate. The ceremony was simple and brief and affected me powerfully. I fought back tears the entire time. Candace held tightly to my hand throughout the service. Afterward, Candace and I went up to talk to his parents.

"We're sorry for your loss," Candace said to them. "James was a good man."

His father's eyes were swollen and red. "He was a good son," he said. "We were very proud of him."

All I could think to say was, "God bless you." Then I turned away. We left after that. We all went back to Sean's house and sat in the front room in a grief-induced stupor. Gone was our usual banter and laughter. Sean brought out a bottle of bourbon and poured us shots. As we finished the bottle, I said to Sean, "We're going to Europe with you."

Candace looked at me. "What?"

"We're going to Europe with them," I said.

Even with her grief, she looked distressed. "Can we talk about this?"

"No. I've made up my mind."

"I can't afford to go to Europe."

"You don't need to," I said. "I've got a trust fund. I'm bringing you."

She looked at me for a moment, then said, "You can't do that."

"Yes I can," I said. "Look at James. He postponed his life and never got the chance to live it. We don't have time to waste. We need to start living now." I turned back to Sean. "I'm going. Final answer."

"Bravo," Sean said.

Candace sighed. "Well, if you're going, I'm going with you."

"Then it's settled," I said. "We're both going. All that's left to do is to tell my father."

CHAPTER

Fourteen

Today I broke my father's heart.

 Luke Crisp's Diary •

Phoenix is a furnace in summer, but as I pulled into the parking lot of Crisp's headquarters, I think I was sweating as much from my nerves as from the heat. My father had built the seven-story building two years before I left for Wharton and had filled the whole of it with Crisp's operations. For the first time in my life I felt uneasy walking through the front doors of the business.

It had been nearly a year since I'd seen my father. I wasn't sure how he would react to my decision to abandon Crisp's for an indulgent excursion around Europe for an indefinite period of time, but I was fairly certain that it wouldn't be received well.

I took the elevator to the seventh floor and took a deep breath before stepping out of it. Mary walked around her desk as I entered the office, her arms outstretched to hug me. "Luke, it's so good to see you."

"It's good to see you too," I replied, taking her embrace.

"I'll let your father know you're here. He's just getting off a conference call right now. He's so excited to see you. We all are."

"Me too," I said, thinking my words sounded feigned. "It's good to be home."

As Mary picked up the phone, a voice boomed behind me, "What's wrong with security? They're letting anyone in off the street." I turned around to see a grinning Henry walking into the office. "Welcome back, my boy."

Henry was in his mid-forties, short and athletically built. The last time I'd seen him, he was losing the battle of the bald. Now, magically, he had a full head of hair.

"Nice locks," I said.

"My new rug," Henry said, tilting his head slightly to show off his hairpiece. "I can even swim in it."

"Now you're going to be fighting women off with a stick."

"That's the idea," Henry said. He stuck out his hand. "Congratulations on your graduation. The family's first M.B.A."

"Yeah, well I think they've done pretty well without one."

"Most of the time," Henry said. I had no idea what he meant by the comment but let it slide.

"Luke."

I turned around to see my father standing in the doorway of his office. I was surprised by how different he looked to me—how much older. It had been longer than I realized. He walked slowly across the room. We embraced.

After we parted, I asked, "You feeling okay?"

"I'm great," he said. "Just a little sore from this morning's squash match. Come in, come in. Let's talk."

I followed him into his office and he shut the door behind us. Everything, except my father, looked exactly the same as it had when I left. I sat down in a tucked leather chair in front of his desk, and he walked in front of me, sitting on the edge of his desk. "I'm so proud of you, Luke. Our first M.B.A."

"It's no big deal," I said.

"It's a very big deal," he replied. His eyes were filled with pride. "I've been so excited for your return. And so ready to get started."

I looked at him. "Started?"

A large smile crossed his face. "On the transition. I'm ready to start turning the company over to you."

I knit my fingers together in my lap, not sure what to say. When I didn't speak, his expression turned. "You're not happy about this? I thought you'd be happy . . ."

"I'm not ready."

"Nonsense. You've been ready for years. You were raised in these stores. You know them better than anyone but me—and I'm ready to hand over the reins."

"Dad . . ." I just looked at him. I could see concern cross his face. "Look, I don't want to do this."

My father looked at me without comprehension. "It doesn't have to happen overnight."

"I mean *ever*."

A shadow came over his face. "What do you mean?"

"I don't want to chain myself to Crisp's."

He just looked at me quietly for a moment. "I don't understand. What do you want to do?"

"I want to *live*."

"I still don't understand," he said.

"I want to really live. I want to experience life. I've worked since I was twelve."

He looked confused.

"Did I tell you about my friend, James?" I asked.

My father shook his head. "Your roommate?"

"No, James was another friend of mine. He was a serious guy. Hardworking, very religious. He graduated third in our class."

My father was just staring at me, no doubt wondering what James had to do with our conversation. "No. You never told me about him."

"Graduation night he was killed by a drunk driver."

"I'm sorry to hear that."

"All that work and sacrifice was for nothing," I said. "He wasted his life."

"I wouldn't call that a wasted life."

"Then what would you call it?"

"Anything but wasted. A man who lives an ethical life adds to the whole of the human family—no matter how brief that life might be."

"You're an idealist, Dad. But the bottom line is, he could have enjoyed his life, instead of spending all those hours at the library poring over his books for nothing." I slowly shook my head. "I used to believe that that was how life was supposed to be. But I don't anymore. Life is meant to be lived, not sweated away. I'm not that kind of fool."

"You mean a fool like me."

"You're twisting my words," I said. "You're no one's fool.

You've lived your life the way it worked for you. I just want to do the same."

My father didn't reply.

"When you insisted that I leave Arizona, you said it was because you didn't want me to have any regrets. You said that you wanted me to see the bigger picture. At the time I didn't want to go, but you were right. I've seen the bigger picture. And the world's a whole lot bigger than the biggest corporate suite. Isn't this what you were trying to teach me? To fly? To live life without regrets?"

My father just looked at me quietly. "And what do I do with the company?"

"Sell it," I said. "Cash in on all your hard work. You could finally be free from Crisp's and enjoy your life."

"You make Crisp's sound like a prison sentence."

"Isn't it?"

After a moment he said: "No. And I've never considered selling it. This has always been a family business. For you, maybe someday for your children."

"What if I don't want it?"

He slowly shook his head. "I could never just walk away. Crisp's is a family. Some of my employees have devoted their entire careers to working for me. I can't just turn them over to someone else. I need to make sure they're taken care of."

"That's part of the problem, Dad. Crisp's *isn't* a family. And it's not a charity. It's a business. If I learned one thing from my M.B.A., it's that. When you forget those boundaries, people will occupy your every waking moment. They'll suck you dry.

"One of my professors used to be the CEO of a major cosmetics company. He told us that he realized it was time to leave when more of his time was spent taking care of his employees' problems than the actual business. Selling Crisp's will be the best thing you've ever done. You'll see that there's another world out there—one you deserve before it's too late to enjoy."

"Eat, drink and be merry for tomorrow we may die," my father said softly.

"Not *may*, Dad. *Will*. Like James. Like Mom."

What I said pierced him. My father looked down for a minute before speaking. "What do you plan to do?"

"For now I'm going to travel with my friends."

"For how long?"

"I don't know. Until I'm done."

"How will you fund this?"

"I have my trust fund."

"And when that runs out?"

"There's a million dollars. It's not running out."

"Money always runs out. A million dollars doesn't go as far as you think."

"It will go far enough," I said.

He looked down at his desk. "I can't stop you from accessing it, but I'm against it."

"I'm sorry, Dad. But this is something I need to do."

He looked perplexed. "I've spent my life creating something to leave to you."

"And you've succeeded. But you've given me something much greater than a company. You've given me freedom."

He threaded his fingers together and put them in front of his mouth, his eyes closed. He looked like he was praying. He stayed that way for a full minute before he looked at me again. He took a deep breath then exhaled slowly.

"Okay," he said. "Follow your own drum. But be careful, son."

"I don't want to live careful," I said. "That's part of the problem, people cling so tightly to their lives that they squeeze the joy out of it. I just want to live."

"I just don't want to see you hurt."

"You won't."

His eyes welled up, which I could see embarrassed him. "I was so excited for your return."

"I'm sorry, Dad."

He took a deep breath. "I can't talk you into sticking around?"

I slowly shook my head.

"Then I suppose there's nothing more to be said. You know how to get the money, I assume."

"I'll visit Mike." I got up and walked to the door. I looked back at him. "Bye," I said.

He was overcome by emotion and couldn't speak. He just nodded.

I quickly walked out of his office and left the building. Whether to fly or fall, I had definitely left the nest.

CHAPTER

Fifteen

Unless you're an engineer, a doctor or mathematician,
the true measure of any decision is less result than intent.

Luke Crisp's Diary

I was about to pull my car out of my parking stall when Henry knocked on my window. I put the car in park and rolled down the window.

"What just happened?" he said. "I haven't seen your father that distressed since your mother passed away."

"I told him that I don't want to run the business."

Henry looked a little surprised but nodded sympathetically. "I can understand. That's a heavy mantle."

"That's what I told him. But he didn't take it very well."

"No, I suppose he wouldn't. He's been planning on you taking over for years. Maybe since you were born."

"Do you think he'll be okay?"

"Your father? Of course he will. He's a survivor. You don't build a *Fortune* 500 company without contingency plans."

"Henry, you know him. Why does he do it? Why does he keep running the company? He could enjoy life, see the world, find love."

"You know, I've asked him that very thing, but he's never given me a straight answer. I'm not sure he has one. Your father came from a different place than you or me. He came from a world of scarcity—where a man fought against the wilderness to survive. But even more than that, your father's a do-gooder. He's been the company nursemaid for thirty years."

"I know. I told him that Crisp's isn't a charity. He should sell the company, take his winnings and move on."

"I've told him that very thing, but he won't listen— improve the P&L, sell, then really start living life. He could buy a yacht and sail around the world." Henry cocked his head. "Who knows, maybe coming from you he'll listen."

"Maybe," I said.

"So what are you going to do now?" Henry asked.

"I'm going to start living. Travel."

"Do you know where you're going?"

"Everywhere. We'll start in New York, then we're headed to Europe"

"Good for you, Luke. Just be safe. And don't worry about a thing. I'll take care of your father."

"Thanks," I said.

He slapped the roof of my car. "Don't mention it. And don't worry. Everything will be just fine."

*

I called Candace from the road. "How'd it go?" she asked.

"Not well," I said. "My father was planning on me taking over the company immediately. I really hurt him."

"I'm sorry."

"Me too. He didn't deserve that."

After a moment she said, "Hurry to New York. I miss you."

"I miss you too," I said.

"Sean went ahead and booked our room on his credit card."

"Tell him thanks. I won't have my new credit card for a few days."

"Just a minute," Candace said, "Sean wants to talk to you."

"You owe me, man," Sean said.

"I know. I'll pay you back."

"How'd it go with the old man? Like you expected?"

"Worse. He was expecting me to take over immediately."

"I told you. It's archetypical. Atlas tries to hand the world over to Hercules. Only you were smart enough to reject it."

"I don't feel that smart right now."

"But he's not stopping you from leaving."

"No. The trust fund is in my name, so there's nothing he can do about it anyway. I just hate disappointing him."

"You'll be feeling better soon enough," Sean said, "Don't worry about your father. It's not what he expected, but he'll come around. He wants you to be happy, right?"

"And if he doesn't come around?" I asked.

Sean laughed. "You'll burn that bridge when you get to it."

⋆

I drove to the office of Mike Semken, our family accountant, and let him know that I was leaving town and needed to access my trust fund. He said it might take a few days to secure a debit card for the account, but he'd have it sent to me as soon as it arrived.

Leaving Semken's office, I stopped at a pub some of the Crisp's employees and I used to frequent and had a drink to settle my nerves. Then I drove to Sky Harbor airport and caught a flight to New York to meet up with the rest of the gang.

✦

The five of us, Candace and I, Sean, Marshall and Lucy, had booked rooms at the Four Seasons Hotel between Park and Madison avenues. I arrived before they did and slept until Candace knocked on my door. She put her arms around me.

"You okay, honey?"

"I'll be okay."

She looked into my eyes. "We're here, so let's be happy." She kissed me. "I'll take good care of you. I promise."

✦

Not surprisingly, Sean knew the Big Apple to the core—from the best restaurants to the most exclusive clubs. He even knew the best hamburger joint, a peculiar dive hidden behind a curtain in the lobby of Le Parker Méridien Hotel off Fifty-Sixth Street.

Candace and I spent the day sightseeing, and that evening we met up with the group and dined at a restaurant called

Per Se, where we sat at a table overlooking Central Park. Candace and I shared a fixed-price tasting menu for $295— which didn't include the wine.

"This is too expensive," Candace said, setting down her menu.

"Actually, Sean's paying for it," I said.

He pointed a finger at me. "You're paying me back."

"Don't worry, I'll have my card in a few days."

"It's still too expensive," Candace said.

"Not for us," I replied.

"But . . ."

I stopped her. "We're going to do this right. I don't want to hear another word about money. I've got plenty. You and I are going to *really* live."

Candace didn't look convinced but acquiesced. "Okay. I won't say another word. I just feel bad spending your money."

"That's right, it's my money." I touched a finger to her lips. "Not another word. No more looking at price tags. Just enjoy. Promise me."

She breathed out slowly. "I promise."

✦

The next day Candace and I spent most of the afternoon at the Metropolitan Museum of Art, then dined at Jean Georges at 1 Central Park West. At Sean's insistence Candace and I chose Chef Vongerichten's seven-course assortment: egg caviar, caramelized cauliflower with a caper-raisin emulsion, young garlic soup with thyme, and a slew of other delicacies I'd never even heard of, let alone tasted.

Culinary indulgences weren't a big part of my upbringing. My father had simple tastes and would be just as happy with a good potato salad as a tin of Beluga caviar. Actually, probably more so. Sean was exposing me to a whole new world.

Our final full day in Manhattan, I took Candace shopping on Fifth Avenue. We stopped at the flagship Apple store, FAO Schwarz (Candace wanted a stuffed animal), Saks, Prada and Louis Vuitton, where I purchased some luggage for our European adventure. We ended the spree in Tiffany's, where I bought Candace a silver chain just so she could have the robin's-egg-blue box. Then I sent her back to the hotel and went to Harry Winston to buy her an emerald-cut diamond solitaire ring. I wasn't sure when I was going to pop the question, but there was no doubt in my mind that it would be sometime during our excursion and I wanted to be prepared.

Lucy was sick when she arrived in New York and spent most of the time in bed. Candace and I were pretty unimpressed with Marshall's care of her, which amounted to almost nothing. Our second-to-last night in New York, Candace scolded him for his neglect.

"What am I supposed to do?" he countered angrily. "Sit around the room with her? She's got room service. What else does she need?"

✦

Our final night in New York everyone, including Lucy, ate at Le Bernardin in the theater district, then attended a Broadway show, *Mamma Mia!* At its conclusion, Sean loudly announced for the benefit of our fellow attendees that the show was "a nauseatingly pedestrian production calculated to take money from bitter, middle-aged women." Also, he wanted to sue the producers for his time back.

CHAPTER

Sixteen

So begins my great adventure abroad.
Here's an applicable quote I found:

"If you actually look like your passport photo,
you're probably not well enough to travel."

Luke Crisp's Diary

From New York, the five of us flew out of JFK to Charles de Gaulle airport in Paris. International travel was an adventure for me. Outside of a two-day business trip my father took me on to Montreal when I was ten, I had never been outside the United States.

From Paris we took a commuter flight to Saint-Tropez, a coastal yacht town along the French Riviera and a vacation spot for celebrities. The small town was an artist's pallet of colors, with yellow, orange and green storefronts and fashionable boutiques set against the brilliant blue of the sea.

Not surprisingly, Sean was as much at home in France as he was in Philadelphia, New York City, or any town for that matter. He was our travel guide and had booked rooms for us at the Château de la Messardière, a five-star hotel perched on a hillside above Pampelonne Bay. Our room had a balcony that overlooked the white sand beach.

"Look at all the lavender," Candace said, leaning over the hotel balcony. I had never seen her so excited before. "Isn't this beautiful?"

I thought that *she* was the most beautiful thing in view.

She was wearing a light sundress, and the ocean breeze gently tossed the fabric as well as her hair. I looked at her, then out over the bay in satisfaction. "*This* is living."

"I've always wanted to come here," Candace said. "This is where Brigitte Bardot was discovered. They say there are more famous faces per meter in Saint-Tropez than anywhere else in the world."

I looked down at the beach below us to the sea of bronzed sunbathers. "Wouldn't surprise me," I said, "Look at all the beautiful people."

"You," she said, taking my chin in her hand and turning my face back toward her, "keep your eyes on me. There's not enough collective fabric down there to make a dishcloth."

We kissed, then I went to the bed and lay down. Candace picked up a tour book from the table, thumbed through it for a while then turned back to me. "A euro for your thoughts."

"I was wondering what my father would think if he saw me now."

"What do you think he'd think?"

"I'd like to think he might be proud that I was seeing the world. But I don't know."

"Give it time," she said.

I sprawled out on the bed, pulling the pillow under my head. "We've got lots of that now."

She sat on the bed next to me and rubbed my back. "Do you mind if I get a pedicure?"

"Of course not. I'm just going to crash. I'm feeling jet-lagged."

There was a knock. Candace walked over and opened the

door to Sean, who was leaning against the frame. "Hi," Candace said. "What room are you guys in?"

"We haven't checked in yet," he said. "I need to talk to Luke."

"Have at him," Candace said, as she stepped past him.

"Hey, brother," Sean said. He walked inside and shut the door behind himself.

"What's up?" I asked.

"I need to borrow your Visa. My card's not working."

I looked at him. "Why isn't your card working?"

"I don't know. But it's still too early in America to call my mother. They won't let us check in without a card."

"I thought you were sharing a suite with Marshall and Lucy."

"I am."

"Why doesn't Marshall put it on his card?"

"Because he's maxed out his allowance, so he's borrowing from me until the end of the month. And he's paying for Lucy."

"So I'm paying for all of you," I said.

"Pretty much," Sean replied.

"Tell them to put it on my card," I said.

"I already tried that. You have to go down and tell them in person."

Something about the casual manner in which he said this bothered me. "You tried to charge it to my card?"

"Of course, you still owe me from New York."

"I know," I said. I got up and followed him down to the

lobby. Downstairs, Marshall was sitting back on a couch looking at a French magazine. Lucy was standing near the front counter watching everyone's luggage. She looked pale, which didn't surprise me, as the last flight had been a little turbulent.

I gave the front desk my credit card and checked them in. I handed out keys, then we walked together toward the elevator. Lucy was struggling with her bags. Neither of the men offered to help her, so I took one of her bags from her.

"Thanks," Lucy said, "Chivalry is not dead."

"No," Marshall said. "Just terminally wounded by the women's movement."

Lucy didn't even look at him.

"So, what are we doing this afternoon?" I asked.

"I've got it planned," Sean said. "First we're headed down to La Tarte Tropézienne. It's the finest pastry shop in Saint-Tropez. Maybe one of the best in France. It's the birthplace of the cream-filled Tarte Tropézienne."

How does he know these things? I thought.

"Then tonight we're going to the exclusive Les Caves du Roy. The place is fantastic—think Las Vegas meets a French grotto. The price to get in is being beautiful." He turned to Marshall. "You might have to stay home tonight."

Marshall shook his head. "Whatever."

"Unlike America," Sean said. "People here actually know how to dance."

✦

Les Caves du Roy is one of France's most famous nightclubs. Sean was right about the club's exclusivity and there were ill-tempered, muscle-bound guards posted at the club's entrance to keep paparazzi away from the celebrities who frequented the establishment. I don't know how Sean did it, but he got us in. The club was decorated in an oriental style with baroque columns wrapped in gold brocade. There were a lot of private nooks and corners. Lucy's eyes were wide as silver dollars. "I think I see Bono," she said.

"Where?" Marshall asked.

"Over there."

"Where?"

"That guy sitting at the table next to the wall."

"That's not Bono," Marshall said snidely. "He looks nothing like him."

Lucy kept staring. "Or maybe it's Sting."

"Bono and Sting don't look anything alike."

"Well, maybe that's because he's in disguise."

Marshall rolled his eyes. "It's a good thing I like dumb women."

True to his original plan, Sean got so drunk that Candace and I ended up taking him back to the hotel. He threw up in the taxi, which warranted a fit from the driver. I don't speak French, but I didn't need to to understand what he was saying. I ended up tipping him 50 euros just to quiet him down.

The next week or so, Candace and I spent most of our time on the beach away from the others, tanning, reading and drinking champagne or Cognac—though Candace was mostly into the fruity drinks, including one called the Saint-

Tropez. At night we'd meet up with the rest of the group for some exotic dinner.

It was the afternoon of our tenth day in Saint-Tropez when Sean came looking for me on the beach. I was alone, reading a Vince Flynn thriller. Candace had gone back to the room an hour earlier to shower and book us a restaurant for dinner.

"Time to leave," Sean said. He was out of breath and strangely overdressed, wearing a beret and dark Vuarnet sunglasses.

"What are you talking about?"

His voice pitched. "I'm serious. We've got to go. I have a car waiting for us."

Even with his eyes hidden behind sunglasses, his anxiety was evident. It was the first time I had ever seen him ruffled.

"We just need to leave. I'll explain later."

I looked at him for a moment then said, "Where are we going?"

"Cannes. It's less than a hundred kilometers from here. Hurry, the car's waiting."

His insistence annoyed me. "Look, Candace and I will just meet you there."

"No, that won't work," he said quickly. "We've all got to go together."

I looked at him, wondering what he was up to. He clearly was motivated by something. "All right. I'll get Candace."

"The car's parked on the street south of the hotel. Come out the south door and walk down to the street."

"Why don't you just have the car waiting out front?"

"We can't do that."

"What's going on, man?"

"Nothing," he said. "We've just got to go. Where's Candace?"

"She's in the room."

"Tell her we have twenty minutes. Remember, don't go out through the lobby. Go out the back door and take the walk to the next street, near the bakery we stopped at yesterday."

"I need to check out."

"No!" he blurted out. He must have realized how anxious he sounded because his voice calmed. "You can do it online from Cannes. *Don't* go down to the lobby."

"It will take us a few minutes," I said. "We're not packed."

"Just hurry," he said. "Please." He looked around, then walked on past me.

More surprising than the conversation, was that he had actually said *please*.

I signed our beachside bar tab, gathered up my things, then went up to our room. Candace was in the bathroom putting on makeup. "Hi, honey," she said. "I got us courtyard reservations at Auberge des Maures. The concierge says we have to try the lamb."

"We'll have to try it later," I said. "Apparently we're leaving town. Sean has a car downstairs waiting for us."

She came out of the bathroom. "What?"

"Sean says we have to go."

"Why?"

"I don't know, but something's wrong. He's scared. Really scared."

"Scared of what?"

I shook my head. "No idea."

"Why don't they just go without us?"

"I said that, but he said we all have to leave. The way he said it made me nervous."

"Do you think someone's after him?"

"It's possible."

She went back into the bathroom. "Probably a jealous husband."

"Whoever it is, he's shaken."

✦

We packed our things and slipped out the back of the hotel as Sean had insisted. Lucy waved to us as we approached the van. The driver quickly put our luggage in back, then we climbed in. Sean was slumped down in the back seat, looking as nervous as a gazelle in lion country. As soon as we were inside, Sean said to the driver, "Let's go. *Dépêche-toi*."

The car pulled out quickly, making its way through the colorful city to the highway. Oddly, none of us said anything about our abrupt departure, though I noticed Sean looking in the driver's rearview mirror a few times. I looked back myself, wondering if we were being followed—wondering what he'd gotten himself, and maybe us, into. Only when we were on the highway did he relax. "You're going to love Cannes," he said softly. "The film festival is over, but the celebrities usually hang out for a couple weeks after."

"We're going to see famous people?" Lucy asked.

"You can count on that," Sean said. "Lots of famous people."

I looked over at Candace. She looked at me and shrugged. I wondered if we'd ever find out what had happened.

CHAPTER

Seventeen

We are living the life of celebrity.

 Luke Crisp's Diary

On the way to Cannes, Sean informed us that the celebrities who came for the festival stayed in yachts or five-star hotels, like the one he had booked for us—the InterContinental Carlton Cannes. The hotel was built in 1911 and was located on the famous Promenade de la Croisette, close to the festival.

As we checked in, the clerk handed me a payment form to sign. I almost gasped when I saw the room rate. "Excuse me," I said. "Is this correct?"

"Is what correct?" he asked with a heavy French accent.

"The price."

"Yes, sir. That is the correct price of the room."

The suites were nearly 2,800 euros a night—nearly $4,000. I turned to Sean. "Did you know it was this much?"

He shrugged. "It's Cannes," he said, as if that explained everything.

What made it worse was that I was still paying for Sean & Company. On the way to Cannes, Sean informed me that he still hadn't worked out his credit card problem. He said his mother was an imbecile when it came to money, and it could be another week before the issue was resolved.

The man at the hotel counter looked annoyed. "Is there a problem, sir?"

"No," I said. I signed the form.

The bellmen took our bags up to our rooms, then we all met at the Carlton Bar on the main floor.

"Our suite is beautiful," Candace said. "We have a seaside view."

"Which suite are you in?" Lucy asked.

"The Grace Kelly."

"We're in the Cary Grant," Lucy said. "They're incredible."

"So are the prices," I said, still reeling from sticker shock.

"The price does include butler and maid service," Marshall said. "You get what you pay for."

What I paid for, I thought.

"Did you see the people lined up outside the hotel?" Sean asked. "They stand there all day waiting to get a glimpse of celebrities. One woman asked me for my autograph."

"I don't suppose you told them that you're not a celebrity," Candace said.

"Why would I do that?" Sean said. "I'll be meeting up with her later tonight."

Candace shook her head. "I saw a real celebrity," she said.

"Who?" Lucy asked.

"Matt Damon."

"Damon! Where?" Lucy said, jumping up from her seat.

"He's gone," Candace said. "He was just getting into a car as we were coming in."

"Why didn't you tell me?"

"Because I know you. I didn't want you to embarrass yourself. Or us."

As usual, Marshall just shook his head.

"What's that you're drinking?" I asked Sean.

"It's a Lady Carlton cocktail. It's named after an English woman who lived in this hotel for twenty-five years."

Twenty-five years at this rate, they should have named the entire hotel after her.

※

We only stayed in Cannes for four nights, which, considering the cost, I was glad for. Sean still hadn't gotten his credit card problem worked out, but he assured me daily that everything would soon be remedied.

From Cannes we drove to Monte Carlo, where we stayed at the Hôtel de Paris, a legendary palace located on Monaco's Place du Casino.

Sean wanted to book the Churchill suite, the hotel's most expensive room, which I vetoed. The junior suite with a casino view was already more than a thousand euros a night—still a bargain compared to our rooms in Cannes.

Less than an hour after checking in, Sean paid me a visit. "Hey, can you spot Marshall and me five K?"

"For?"

"I'm going to play a little Chemin de Fer."

Candace was standing next to me, looking at Sean skeptically.

He smiled. "Look, it's a good deal for you," he said. "If

I lose, I pay you back. If I win, I'll split my winnings with you. How do you beat that?" Then he added. "Same goes for Marshall."

"What about Lucy?" Candace asked.

"She's staying in the room. She's sick again."

"We'll take her to dinner," Candace said.

"I doubt she'll be up for it. She's been tossing her cookies for the last half hour."

"Why isn't Marshall staying with her?" Candace asked.

Sean grinned. "Like that's going to happen."

I took out my wallet and brought out a wad of bills. "I've got four thousand," I said.

"Four will do. Thanks, amigo." He started to turn but stopped. "Wait, I'm going to need a little extra. The casino's got a dress code and I didn't bring a jacket. Maybe I should just take your credit card. There's an Armani store a block from the hotel."

"You with my credit card," I said. "I may be crazy, but I'm not dumb."

He waved me off. "Never mind. I'm sure they'll have a jacket closet."

"Look," I said, "you're keeping a record of all this money, right?"

He smiled. "I thought you were."

I raised my eyebrows.

"Just kidding. Of course I am. We'll be at the Casino de Monte Carlo if you decide to join us."

"Candace and I are staying in tonight."

"Good for you," he said.

He turned and walked out. I shut the door behind him.

"You've got to stop doling out money for him," Candace said.

"I'm not doling it, I'm loaning it," I said.

"You sure?"

I looked at her gravely. "He's good for it, isn't he?"

"You wouldn't know if he wasn't, would you?"

She had a point. "I guess we'll find out," I said.

CHAPTER

Eighteen

*I've heard it said that if you want to know someone,
travel with them—you'll either end up loving or leaving them.
It might be true.*

✦ Luke Crisp's Diary •

We had only been in Monte Carlo for a week when Sean insisted that Paris was calling. As beautiful as Monte Carlo was, I went along with his plans. In part because I was tired of Sean asking for gambling money. But, more importantly, Paris seemed like the ideal place to propose to Candace. Candace and I had grown even closer over the past few weeks, and I was now more certain than ever that I wanted to spend the rest of my life with her.

Sean suggested we stay at the Four Seasons George V, located in one of the most fashionable quarters of Paris and within walking distance of the Arc de Triomphe, the Place de la Concorde and the Eiffel Tower. Candace gasped as we entered the hotel's lobby, which was what I was hoping for. The hotel was decorated with bright tapestries, marble columns and fresh flowers and smelled of geraniums.

"Luke, this is incredible," she said.

"Nothing's too good for my girl," I said.

She leaned into me. "Except you," she replied.

✦

Walking into our room elicited even more excitement from Candace. Our room was decorated with royal blue cloth-covered walls, crystal chandeliers and, like the lobby, fresh flowers.

The room was about $2,500 a night. Looking back, I can see the change that had come over me. In my previous life I would never have considered spending more than a few hundred dollars a day for a hotel room, but the $4,000 suites in Cannes had corrupted my perspective. I actually considered the price of the rooms a bargain. At least I would have if I was paying for just one of them. I had booked two rooms next to each other. I was anxious about still putting Sean's room on my bill. His tab was skyrocketing, and I still hadn't seen any evidence of him fixing his credit card problem or paying me back.

As usual, Sean had prepared our agenda. We ate dinner at *Le Bristol*, a fashionable restaurant that changes its décor with the seasons. It was there that I tasted white truffles for the first time—an aromatic fungus that sometimes costs more per ounce than gold. I could no more describe its taste than describe salt.

The next few days Candace and I separated from the group and visited all the popular attractions that Americans come to Paris for. We took a river cruise on the Seine and spent nearly an entire day at both the Louvre and the Musée d'Orsay.

Our first Friday night in Paris, Sean insisted we visit a popular nightclub in the Champs-Élysées district called Les

Bains Douches, one of the hottest spots in Paris. It ended up just being the three guys, since Candace was tired from the day's walking and Lucy wasn't feeling well again.

"Les Bains Douches means 'The Baths,' " Sean said on the cab ride to the club. "It was built on the site of a Turkish bath."

When we got to the club door, Sean said to me, "Give the man a fifty."

I looked at him. "What for?"

"The bouncers are notorious for turning people away for no reason. If you're not a model or Mick Jagger, you gotta pay to play."

I reluctantly passed the bouncer 50 euros, but we still had to wait nearly forty minutes to get in. That wasn't the worst thing to happen. Not by a long shot. We ate dinner in the club's Thai restaurant, but when the waitress brought us our check, I almost choked. She had put a $1,000 bottle of champagne on our bill.

When I protested the charge, I was immediately surrounded by three bouncers, who strong-armed me to a back room and made me swipe my debit card for the entire amount. My father used to say, "The world is designed to take your money." I was quickly learning how right he was, though some parts of the world are more adept at doing so.

To dull my humiliation, I took to drinking with Marshall. I had no idea where Sean was. The last I'd seen of him he was walking out of the club with his arms around two Italian women.

Around two in the morning, Marshall nudged me with

his elbow. "Luke, check that out." His eyes were fixed on an exotic-looking French woman in a revealing dress. She looked over at him and a seductive smile turned up her lips. He immediately stood. *"Mon bel ange.* That, my friend, is the only thing on earth that could convince me to learn French."

"What about Lucy," I said.

"She doesn't speak French," he said with a condescending smile. "Don't worry about me, I'll find a ride home." He walked across the room to the woman.

I wished I had stayed back with Candace. Actually, I was beginning to wish I had stayed in Arizona. I finished my drink and went back to the hotel.

CHAPTER

Nineteen

Truth is patient. It can afford to be,
for eventually it will have its way.

✦ Luke Crisp's Diary ✦

When I arrived back at the Four Seasons, Lucy was asleep in our room with Candace. I turned on the entryway lights, and Lucy rubbed her eyes then sat up, slowly looking around. "Where's Marshall?" she asked.

"Still out," I said.

She looked at me with a pained expression. "Is he with another woman?"

In spite of my desire to do otherwise, I nodded.

Lucy stood up and went back to her own room. Candace just looked at me and frowned. "Come here, baby," she said.

✦

Several hours later we woke to yelling coming from Lucy and Marshall's room next door. Lucy's voice was punctuated by sobs. I looked over at the clock. It was nearly 5 A.M.

"Have you ever heard her that upset before?" I asked.

"Yes," Candace said. "It's their cycle."

There was another loud scream followed by louder crying. Then I heard a door slam.

"I think the chain just fell off their cycle," I said.

"Will you check on her?" Candace asked.

"Sure." I pulled on a pair of sweat pants and walked out into the hall. Lucy was lugging her suitcase to the elevator.

"Hey," I said.

She turned around. Her eyes were puffy and red and she was trembling.

"Where are you going?" I asked.

"Anywhere he isn't."

I walked toward her. "Want to talk?"

She wiped her eyes then said, "Yes."

We went back to my room. Candace had put on a robe and she hugged Lucy as she came in. "I'm sorry, honey," she said. "But you've been here before. Things will work out."

"No they won't," she said. "He told me he doesn't love me. He said he hasn't cared about me for more than a year. He's just been using me."

I gently rubbed her back. "Marshall's a jerk. The only person he cares about is himself. You're better off without him."

"No, I'm not," she said.

"You will be," I said. "Trust me. It may not seem like it now, but as soon as you're free from him, you'll be much better off."

She looked up, her eyes darting back and forth between us. "I'm pregnant."

For a moment Candace and I were both silent. Then Candace said, "Oh."

That's why she's been so sick, I thought.

"I don't know what I'm going to do," Lucy said.

"Does he know you're pregnant?" Candace asked.

"I told him tonight. That's what started his yelling. He said I'd gotten pregnant to trap him." Lucy continued to cry. "He said he doubted it was even his baby." She put her head down. "That's when he told me he didn't love me."

I softly caressed her hand. "I'm really sorry. He's an idiot."

"I'm the idiot," she said. "How could I have been so stupid?"

Candace made Lucy stay with us. I laid a blanket across the sofa for myself and Lucy climbed in bed with Candace, though I'm not sure either of the women slept.

Lucy quietly got up a few hours later. She took a quick shower and then came out of the bathroom dressed. "I better go," she said.

"Why don't you just stay with us for a few days?" Candace said.

"No," she said, her voice strained, "I can't be around him."

"Where will you go?"

"Home. I'll go home."

"How will you get back to the states?" I asked.

"I'm not sure. I was going to ask my aunt to send me some money."

I took out my wallet and pulled out ten 100-euro bills. "This will get you home."

She looked at me gratefully. "Thank you." She leaned forward and kissed me on the cheek. "Thank you for being so good to me. I wish I had what you and Candace have."

I walked her down to the lobby and helped her get a cab. When I got back to the room, Candace said, "Think she'll be okay?"

"For now," I said.

"I hate Marshall," she said.

"I know. How could anyone be so cold?"

✦

Later, in the afternoon, Candace, Sean and I were in the hotel's restaurant eating lunch when Marshall walked in. He looked to be in good spirits. "Hey, people," he said flippantly. "Whassup?"

"Lucy went home," I said.

"Yeah, I figured she would." He sat down at the table and lifted a menu. "So what's good?"

Candace and I looked at him incredulously. "You're not bothered by this?" Candace asked.

He didn't even look up from the menu. "Why would I be? She's not my problem."

"She's pregnant," Candace said.

"Yeah, well she should have done a better job protecting herself."

"Stunning," Candace said. "After all this time together, you just toss her like she's trash."

I glanced over at Sean, who seemed more amused than disturbed by the conversation. He hadn't returned to the hotel until 8 A.M., so he'd missed Lucy and Marshall's fight.

"It's none of your business," Marshall said. "She chose her path."

"You're such a loser," Candace said.

Marshall pointed at her. "Shut your mouth."

"Don't talk to her that way," I said, leaning toward him threateningly. He cowered back. "You're a jerk, Marshall. You always have been. You dress up your selfishness like it's some deep, philosophical statement, but the truth is, you're just a cheater and a user. It's time for you to leave."

He laughed, then turned to Sean. "Can you believe this guy?" He looked back at me. "It's a free country, man."

"Free? No, it's two thousand euros a day."

"I'm not going anywhere, dude."

"Well, I'm not paying your way anymore," I said.

He grimaced. "What are you talking about? You're not paying my way. Sean is."

"Oh, really?" I turned to Sean. "Is that true?"

"I'm going to pay you back," Sean said.

I shook my head. "I'll make it easy on both of you. I'm not giving Sean another euro until you're gone."

"Wow," Sean said, leaning back from the table. "That's harsh."

Marshall looked at Sean for backup. Sean just shrugged. "Sorry, man," he said, "Out of my hands."

Marshall's face turned red. "You're calling *me* a cheater? Did you ever tell Candace about your one-night stand with the UPenn undergrad?"

Candace blanched. She looked at me with a shocked expression.

Marshall grinned. "Didn't think so."

"Is it true?" Candace asked.

I had no idea what to say. When I didn't answer, she stood up and stormed off from the table. I stood and watched her go, debating whether to run after her or not.

"Glass houses and stones," Marshall said. He looked back at Sean. "I need some money to get home."

"I'm broke," Sean said.

Marshall turned to me. "I need some money."

I looked at him, my face red with anger. "You've got to be kidding."

"What am I supposed to do?"

"Not my problem," I said.

CHAPTER

Twenty

How can so few seconds of pleasure
bring so many days of agony?

✦ Luke Crisp's Diary ✦

Candace wouldn't talk to me the rest of the day, and I ended up spending the night in Sean's room. The next morning she opened the door when I knocked. Her eyes were so swollen they were almost closed. She looked like she had cried all night.

"What do you want?" she said.

"I want to tell you how sorry I am. It was so stupid. I had been drinking . . . It was wrong. I love you, Candace. I never wanted to hurt you."

"How many times did you see her?"

"Once. Just the one time. I was so drunk, I don't even know her name."

"Why didn't you tell me?"

"Because I didn't want to hurt you."

"Well, you did."

I exhaled slowly. "I was going to tell you. I felt so guilty. But Sean talked me out of it. He said I was being selfish by trying to assuage my guilt by breaking your heart."

She looked at me incredulously. "And you listened to him?"

I shook my head. "I know, it's stupid. I'm really sorry. I

don't know what else to say. I'm begging you. Please, give me another chance. It will never happen again. I promise."

"And why should I believe you now?"

"Because you know I love you." I looked at her hopefully. "And because you love me."

Her eyes began to well up with tears.

"I'm so sorry," I said.

She wiped her eyes. "I know." She looked at me. "No more secrets."

"No more secrets," I said.

"If you ever do it again, I won't give you another chance."

"It won't happen again."

She let me back in the room. So much for romantic Paris.

CHAPTER

Twenty-One

We haven't seen Sean for days.
Neither of us has suggested sending out a search party.

✦ Luke Crisp's Diary ✦

I was through with France. We'd lost Lucy and Marshall, and, frankly, with Sean now owing me more than $50,000 I wouldn't have been too upset to lose him too. Worst of all, I had almost lost Candace. I had planned to propose to her in Paris, and now I was just lucky that she hadn't flown home. I hoped that Italy would bring a different fate.

✦

The next morning the three of us flew from Paris to Rome. Sean was hungover from a final night of partying and Candace was quiet most of the way.

Sean suggested we stay at the Residenza Napoleone III, which is exactly what it sounds like—the hotel had been the residence of Emperor Napoleon III during the 1830s. Considering the price of the place, I probably would have found someplace else if it wasn't for what Candace and I had just gone through. I wanted her to be someplace special.

✦

We didn't see much of Sean the next week. I don't know where he went, but we didn't miss him. We needed the time alone to set things right. We took in the usual sights: the Colosseum and the Forum, the Spanish Steps, and the Trevi Fountain. We spent a day at Vatican City where we listened to a choir in St. Peter's Basilica and followed a guide through the Sistine Chapel. By our third day, things between us felt good again.

We dined in three piazzas: Piazza Navona with its Bernini fountains, Piazza del Popolo with its Egyptian obelisk, and Piazza di Spagna with its marble boat churning with fresh water. By the end of our first week in Italy, we decided we'd seen enough of Rome and made plans to leave the next day by train. We planned to go to Florence, Bologna, and then Venice. We still hadn't seen Sean and frankly I was ready to just leave him.

We had been asleep for several hours when someone pounded on our door. I checked the time on the electric alarm clock: 2:46. I turned on the lamp on the nightstand next to me and walked to the door. I looked through the door's peephole and saw Sean standing there.

"We're sleeping. Go away."

"Luke, open up. It's urgent."

Surprisingly, he didn't sound drunk. "Just a minute," I said. I walked over to the closet and put on a robe.

Candace woke. "Who's at the door?"

"It's Sean," I said.

"What time is it?"

"Almost three."

"Tell him to go away."

"I did." I walked back to the door, opening it a crack. "C'mon, Sean. It's two forty-five. Come back in the morning."

"Please," he said. His voice was pitched and nervous—just as it had been in Saint-Tropez. I opened the door and looked out. I didn't understand what I saw. Sean was leaning against our door's threshold. He was pale and his forehead was beaded with sweat. His hand was wrapped in a white cloth stained with blood. Even more peculiar, there were two men standing about twenty feet from him on both sides of the hall.

"What's going on? What happened to your hand?"

"They found me," he said.

"Who found you?" I looked back and forth between the two men. "Them?"

"They're going to kill me."

"What are you talking about?"

"Come back to bed," Candace said. "Tell Sean to come back in the morning." She rolled over.

I stepped out into the hall. "What's going on?"

Sean said, "Remember back in Saint-Tropez when we had to leave? I was gambling and I went too far. They've followed us all the way here."

"Who followed you?"

"Some men I met at a bar."

"How much did you lose?"

"Two hundred."

"They followed you here for two hundred dollars?"

"Two hundred *thousand*."

His words stunned me. "You lost two hundred thousand dollars?"

"Euros."

"Euros. That's almost three hundred thousand dollars."

"I'm sorry, man. But you've got to help me. I need the money."

"Sean, you're already in to me at least fifty grand."

"You know I'm good for it."

"No, I don't know that." I shook my head. "That's too much money. You need to call your father."

"He wouldn't give it to me."

"He would if he knew your life was at stake."

"Then he definitely wouldn't give it to me," Sean said.

"Then call your mother."

He looked at me fearfully. "She's cut me off too."

"What?"

"She's cut me off."

Now I had real reason to be concerned. "You didn't tell me that. You lied to me."

"I can get the money from my uncle. But it will take a little time." He leaned close, his eyes wide with fear. "You've got to help me, man. If I don't have the money by morning, they're going to cut off my fingers. If I don't have it by tomorrow night, they'll kill me."

I looked back at the two men. I didn't doubt that they were capable of violence. "You need to call the police."

Sean's eyes flashed with panic. "Are you kidding? My life would be worth nothing." I noticed his hands were shaking. "Please, Luke. Don't let them kill me. I'm begging you."

I ran my fingers back through my hair. "You're talking three hundred thousand dollars."

"You know they'll kill you and Candace too," he said.

My chest constricted. "We don't have anything to do with this."

"They know we're together. If they kill me, you and Candace are witnesses."

"How do they know about me and Candace?"

"They're right there, man," he squeaked. "These guys tracked us from France. They know everything about us. You've got to get me the money. It's our only way."

I glanced at the men, then back at Sean. "You stupid, lying fool," I said. "You're going to pay me back every penny."

"Every penny. I promise." He looked back at the men who were staring at us. "You have to tell them what's going on."

"All right," I said. "Which one's in charge."

"That guy," Sean said, turning back to one side. I walked over to him with Sean. The man at the other end of the hall walked up to us. The men looked at us with a darkness that literally sent a chill through me.

"I'm going to help him out," I said. "But we'll have to wait for the bank to open."

The smaller of the two men spoke in a thick accent I didn't recognize. "There bank on Via Condotti. We be at bank at eight-thirty. If you not come bank, we kill friend. If you tell police, we kill friend and you."

"There won't be any problem," I said, "I'll get you the money."

The man looked at his partner. He grabbed Sean by his arm and yanked him back. "You hope he have money."

Sean looked at me fearfully. "He'll get the money."

"Don't be late to bank," the man said to me.

✦

I didn't sleep the rest of the night. I got up around eight. Candace was still asleep, but she woke as I was looking for my passport. I couldn't believe how crazy this was. I couldn't believe that I was dealing with people like this—this was something that happened in movies, not my life. I was furious at Sean for dragging us into this. Part of me wanted to let Sean suffer the consequences of his actions for once—but I had no doubt they'd kill him, and even as angry as I was at Sean, he didn't deserve that.

As I was putting on my shoes, Candace stirred. "Where are you going?"

I walked over to the bed and knelt down next to her. "It's early. I couldn't sleep," I said. "I thought I'd just walk around."

"I'll come with you," she said.

"No, it's too early. Go back to sleep."

She yawned. "You sure?"

"Yeah. Just sleep."

"Okay." She rolled back over.

I gathered my things then walked out of the room. I took a cab to the bank the men had directed me to. The men were parked in a car across the street in a Fiat Punto. One of the men got out of the car as I approached. He said nothing as we walked into the bank. I could see Sean in the back seat.

✦

I hadn't considered that the banks in America would still be closed when I went to make the transfer. I explained to the men the problem, then I waited around until nearly three in the afternoon to try again. My stomach was in knots. The process of transferring the funds took nearly an hour, and it was almost four o'clock when Sean and I got back to the hotel. Not surprisingly, Candace was frantic. She was waiting for us in the hotel lobby.

"Where have you been? I've been terrified that something happened to you."

"I had some financial matters I needed to . . ." I said.

"No more secrets!" she shouted. "And don't talk to me like I'm an idiot! I've got an M.B.A. What kind of financial matters?"

"I needed to borrow some money," Sean said.

"What else is new? And that takes eight hours?"

"Two hundred thousand euros," I said.

Her mouth opened in a partial gasp. "What?"

"Sean got in with some gamblers in Saint-Tropez and they followed us here."

"They were bad dudes," Sean said.

"They were going to kill him if he didn't come up with the money."

She glared at Sean, then back at me. "You should have let them," she said. She turned and stormed back to our room.

When she was gone, I said to Sean, "We're leaving."

"I know where we can go next," he said. "Dubai. I have a friend who has connections. We can get a room at the Burj-al-Arab for just twelve hundred a night for a month's stay."

I just looked at him. "Does any of this even faze you?"

"Any of what?"

I shook my head. "Candace is right, I should have let them have you. We're going back to the States. I'm sick of the drama and I'm sick of being bled dry by you."

"I'll get you the money," Sean said. "I told you I would. Where are you going?"

"Someplace warm."

"My uncle lives in Vegas," Sean said. "We can go there and I'll get you the money."

I really wanted to leave him. Looking back, I should have—but when someone owes you as much money as Sean did, you want to keep him close.

Twenty-Two

The Bible says that money has wings.
It doesn't. It has rocket engines.

✦ Luke Crisp's Diary ✦

The next afternoon we flew from Rome to Atlanta to Las Vegas. I was glad to be back in the States. Candace seemed relieved as well. Now all we needed was to get my money back, then dump Sean.

I booked two regular rooms at the Bellagio and Candace and I went right to bed, waking at ten the next morning. Candace was showering when Sean knocked on our door. I put on my robe and answered.

"Good news," he said, walking into the room with his usual grin.

"You talked to your uncle," I said.

"No, better, man. I landed a cabana at the Rehab."

"Rehab," I said. "You're finally seeing someone for your drinking problem?"

Sean laughed. "You're an idiot. Rehab is the pool at the Hard Rock Hotel & Casino. It's world-famous for their epic pool parties. Just think, two thousand buzzed beautiful women."

"You're broke," I said. "How did you pay for it?"

"I charged it to my room."

"You charged it to me? How much did it cost?"

"Are you even listening to me? Do you have any idea how

much schmoozing it took to get a cabana on a Friday afternoon? You should kiss my feet."

"How much?" I repeated.

"Three grand," he said.

"Cancel it."

"I can't. It's nonrefundable. That's how I got the deal."

"I want my money," I said. "You talk to your uncle today."

"Chill, man. I'll get it."

I shut the door on him. Candace came out of the bathroom wrapped in a towel. "What does he want now?"

"He just rented a cabana at some place called the Rehab."

"I've seen it on TV," Candace said.

"It was three grand," I said.

Candace said, "You've got to dump him."

"Tomorrow," I said. "He comes up with my money or he's gone."

"So we're going to the Rehab? Do you mind if I do a little shopping over at the Venetian? I need a bikini."

"No, I'll come with you. I've got to get out of this place."

✳

After Candace had purchased a swimsuit and cover-up, we walked over to the Wynn Las Vegas. I stopped outside the Rolex shop to look at one of the watches in the display window.

"I've always wanted one of those," I said to Candace, pointing at a Rolex President. I looked at the price tag. "Twenty-two thousand dollars."

"After all you've given everyone else, you deserve to spend a little on yourself. Give me the card, I'll buy it for you."

I handed my card to her and I followed her inside. She purchased the watch and put it on my wrist. "Now you're ready for your cabana."

We took a cab from the Wynn to the Hard Rock Hotel. The Rehab was a massive pool lined with palm trees, cabanas and bikinis. There was probably as much alcohol as water. We were led to our cabana. Sean was already there and, judging by the glasses on the table, well on his way to getting drunk.

I was greeted by a pretty, bikini-clad server. "Hello, Mr. Crisp," she said. "I'm Dot. I'm your cabana girl today. We've already opened a tab for you, may I get you started on some drinks?"

Sean said, "Bring me a Tequila Sunrise."

"I'll have a scotch," I said. "Make it a double."

"I'll have a piña colada," Candace said.

"I'll be right back," she said. As she walked away, I asked Sean, "Did you call your uncle?"

He grimaced. "Don't ruin it. I told you I would."

+

Candace and I sat back in our chairs while Sean roamed the pool like a reef shark. A short time later he returned with a half dozen girls, two of them clinging to his arms.

"Lookie what Daddy brought home," he said.

"Par-teeeee," one of the girls said.

"Hey, girls," Sean said. "This is Luke, your host and bene-factor."

One of the girls, a short, overly tanned woman in a bright orange bikini, sidled up to me. "Hello, Luke. I'm Sam."

Candace took my arm. "And I'm Candace. He's taken."

"You sure?" she said to me, avoiding Candace's glare.

"I'm sure," I said.

Her smile never left. "Whatever." She went back to Sean.

I spent the afternoon watching the women drink my money. Sean kept disappearing with different women.

Last day, I kept telling myself.

By late afternoon, Candace decided that she'd had enough sun—or drunk girls—likely both. "I'm going back to the room," she said.

I had had enough myself. "Me too," I said. "I'll meet you back there. I need to find Dot and close out the tab."

A few minutes later Dot came by to check on us. "Mr. Crisp, can I get you anything?"

"No, I'm fine," I said. Actually, I was furious. I had just watched Sean water a plant with a $100 bottle of wine. As I looked at him, I realized just how much I hated him—and myself for letting him use me.

"I'm ready to close out my bill," I said. "Just put everything on my card."

"I'll be right back," she said.

Less than five minutes later Dot returned. "Mr. Crisp, we have a little problem."

"A problem?"

"Your card was declined."

"Declined?" I said. "That's impossible, it's a debit card."

She shrugged.

"How much is our bill anyway?"

"Nine thousand eight hundred fifty-five dollars."

"Almost ten grand?"

"I can provide you with an itemized receipt. Your friends have been drinking a lot."

"My card still shouldn't have been declined. Can you try it again?"

"It can't hurt." She returned a moment later looking upset. I noticed that a security guard had followed her back.

"It came up declined again," she said. "Do you have another card?"

"No, just that one," I said. "Something's wrong. I need to make a call." With them watching me, I took out my cell phone and dialed Semken's office. His receptionist answered.

"Semken Holmes Accounting."

"I need to speak with Mike."

"I'm sorry, Mr. Semken is in a meeting with a client."

"*I'm* a client," I snapped. "Look, this is Luke Crisp and this is urgent. You're going to have to interrupt his meeting."

"I'm sorry, Mr. Semken asked me not to interrupt him."

"This is an emergency," I shouted. "Tell him that."

She said, "I'll see if he'll take your call."

It was nearly five minutes before Semken answered.

"This is Mike."

"Mike, it's Luke Crisp."

"Luke," he said. "Where in the world are you? And what's the problem?"

"I'm in Vegas."

"There's your problem," he said.

"Look, I just tried to use my debit card and it was declined."

"Let me see what's going on." I could hear him typing on a computer keyboard. "That's because you've exceeded your credit limit."

"Credit limit. It's a debit account. Didn't you transfer all my trust funds?"

"I transferred the balance as you directed. The account is overdrawn. Let's see, you have been making some sizable withdrawals. Here's one alone for two hundred seventy-two thousand seven hundred forty-seven dollars and thirty-two cents."

"But I had more than a million dollars in my trust."

"That's not quite true. You had nine hundred sixty-two thousand, two hundred seventy-four gross, but you had taxes of course, so you really had seven hundred twenty-four thousand five hundred sixty-five."

I knew there would be taxes, but I hadn't really computed it into my behavior—the truth was I hadn't thought that hard about anything.

". . . Then with the fall in the market, you were down to four hundred seventy-nine thousand three hundred sixty-two." He was silent as he reviewed my account. "Looks like you've been traveling in Europe. The dollar's so weak now, the exchange rate was killing you."

I sat in stunned silence. "You're telling me that I'm broke?"

"No, just this account."

"Do I have any other accounts?"

"What do you mean?"

"Do I have anything I can access with money in it? An emergency fund?"

"I have nothing with your name. Your father has accounts, but he would have to authorize the release of those funds. Perhaps you should call your father."

I breathed out heavily, trying not to hyperventilate. "I need your help. I need ten grand right now."

"Of course I'll help you, Luke. Just tell me where to get the money."

"Can you loan me something from one of my father's accounts?"

He laughed. "You know I can't do that."

"My father has invested millions with you."

"And that's because he knows I'll protect his money. I suggest you give him a call. Good luck." He hung up. My father's words came back to me. *Money always runs out.*

The security guard looked angry. *Paris all over again,* I thought. Only this time there was no card to swipe. "I've got a problem," I said.

Dot grimaced. "I'm dead."

"Maybe if you try the card for a lesser amount," I said.

"How much?"

"I don't know. Maybe seven or eight thousand."

"I can try." She came back a few minutes later. "It cleared

for seventy-five hundred. That leaves a balance of two thousand three hundred and fifty-five."

I checked my wallet. All I had was $232. "I need to call some people. I need to go back to my room."

"You're not leaving," the guard said.

"It would be best . . ."

He cut me off. "The only way you leave this place without paying your bill is in a police cruiser," he said.

I pointed at Sean. "Why don't you take him, he's the one doing all the drinking."

"Cabana's in your name, sir," the guard said.

"I got you seventy-five hundred dollars. I'll get you the rest."

"It's resort policy."

As I tried to think of a solution, I remembered my new Rolex. "Can you take my watch as collateral?"

The guard shook his head. "We're not a pawnshop."

"Can I take it back? It will only take me a few minutes."

"You can't leave the resort, sir."

"Can someone come with me?"

"We can't leave the resort, sir."

I looked around, exasperated. I shouted to Sean, "Sean, do you have any money?"

He was kissing one of the women.

"Sean," I shouted again.

He turned to me looking annoyed. "What?"

"Do you have any money?"

"Yeah, right," he said. He turned back to the woman.

I didn't even consider asking him to take my watch back.
He was too hammered and I doubted I would actually see
the money. "Let me call my girlfriend and have her return my
watch." I telephoned Candace, but she didn't answer. I tried
five more times over the next twenty minutes. The security
guard was losing his patience.

"Okay, maybe someone will buy my watch."

The guard followed me as I walked to the cabana next to
ours. I pulled the watch from my arm. "I need to raise some
cash," I said loudly. "I've got a Rolex President I bought this
morning. It's a twenty-two-thousand-dollar watch. I'll sell it
for half that."

They all turned away from me.

"I'll sell it for seven thousand dollars."

"Get lost," someone said.

"Thirty-five hundred," I said.

"Thirty-five hundred," a young man said. "Let me see it."

I couldn't believe I was that desperate. I took the watch
off and handed it to him. He looked it over. "How do I know
it's real?"

"It's real."

"I can tell," another man standing next to him said. He
held it up, studying its movement. "It's real." He handed the
watch back to his friend. The man looked at it again, then
handed it back to me. "I'll give you twenty-eight hundred."

"Come on," I said. "Thirty-five was ridiculously low."

The man shrugged. "Sorry, it's all I got. Take it or leave it."
He turned away.

I looked around. Dot and the security man were staring at me. "All right," I said in exasperation. "Twenty-eight."

The man turned back and said, "Deal." He took out his wallet and counted out a stack of hundreds. I noticed he had more bills in his wallet after counting out the money.

I counted out $2,355 and handed it to Dot. She counted it out as well, then turned to the guard and nodded. He glanced at me and walked away. Dot looked back at me with indignity. "No tip?"

I handed her a $100 bill, which was suddenly a fortune to me but did little to please her since she expected much more from a $10,000 bar tab.

"A hundred dollars?"

"Get the rest from him," I said, pointing at Sean.

She approached Sean. Sean said something to her I couldn't hear, but I saw her throw up her arms, then walk away angrily. Sean must have tried to order a drink from her because he immediately approached me. "What gives, Crispy? She said they've cut off our bar tab."

"I shut it down," I said. "I'm out of money."

"You've got to do something, man. The girls will leave."

"You didn't hear me. I'm *out of money*."

"Then transfer some more into your account."

"There's nothing left to transfer. It's gone. All of it."

He looked at me as if I were speaking Chinese. "You blew through your entire trust fund?" he said, as if he'd had nothing to do with it.

"You owe me money. You need to get it."

"I told you I'd get it."

"I need it now."

"I can't get it right now," he said. "Why don't you just call your dad?"

"Why don't *you* call your dad?" I snapped back.

"I don't have one," Sean said.

"Then call your uncle. You need to call him *now*."

He looked at me with a bizarre grin. "I don't have one of those either."

It was as if the scales fell from my eyes. For the first time I saw Sean for who he really was. I slammed my fist into his face and he dropped to the ground. "You stinking thief," I shouted. "You lying, stinking user."

He held his hand to his bleeding nose. "You hit me." He looked at me from the ground with a twisted grin. "You're a hypocrite, Crisp. Where did you get your money? It was no sweat off your back, man. You used your old man—I used you. It's the circle of life."

"You've got an excuse for everything, don't you, you dirtbag."

Even with blood on his face he smiled. "I told you when we first met," he said. "Cardboard soul, man. Cardboard soul." He stood up, then stumbled off away from me.

Up to that point I hadn't realized I had the capacity to hate someone that much.

CHAPTER

Twenty-Three

*I have pulled the mask from Sean's face to reveal the real man,
only to learn that I preferred him with the mask.*

✦ Luke Crisp's Diary ✦

I had $577 to my name. I took a $12 cab back to the hotel—it was the first time in six months that I'd actually paid attention to the amount—and went up to our room. Candace was lying on the bed.

"Hey," she said as I walked in. "Sorry I missed your calls. I was in the shower."

"We've got to go," I said.

She looked at me quizzically. "Go where?"

"I don't know," I said, sitting on the bed.

She sat up. "What's wrong?"

"Sean's gone," I said. "For good." I rubbed my fist.

"Did he pay you back?"

I grinned darkly. "Yeah, right."

"What about his uncle? Did he call him?"

"Sean doesn't have an uncle."

"What?"

I looked into her eyes. "Candace, I ran out of money."

"What do you mean?"

"My entire trust fund is gone."

She looked at me in shock. "We couldn't possibly have spent that much."

"I didn't have as much as I thought. And between the stock market, the five-star hotels, thirty-dollar martinis, Sean's gambling and the exchange rate, I'm broke."

For a moment she was speechless. "What are we going to do?"

I took a deep breath. "I don't know. Do you have any money?"

"Only a couple hundred. Where's your watch?" she asked.

"I sold it at the Rehab. It's the only way they'd let me out of there," I said. "Do you have any money at home?"

"I've got a couple thousand in an IRA."

"That won't get us far."

Candace looked terrified. "You have to call your father."

"I can't."

"Why?"

I exploded. "Because, I can't."

"So he won't know you failed?"

"He already knows I failed. I failed the minute I left him. And no, I don't want him to see me like this."

Candace stood there mulling over our dilemma. Finally she said, "What are we supposed to do, Luke? Live on your pride?"

"What makes you think he would even want to talk to me?"

"You could at least try."

I sat there looking at her and then threw my hands up in surrender. "Fine," I said. "I'll call."

I took out my phone and dialed my father's cell phone. I wasn't even sure what to say. I didn't have to find out. There was no answer except a recorded message telling me that the number I'd dialed had been disconnected. It made no sense. My father had had the same cellular number since cell phones were the size of lunch boxes. Few people had his personal number. I could think of no reason he would disconnect his phone.

"He's disconnected his phone," I said. I dialed my father's direct number at Crisp's headquarters. A female voice I didn't recognize answered. "Mr. Price's office."

"This is Luke Crisp. Is my father in?"

"Excuse me?"

"Is Carl Crisp in?"

"I'm sorry, Mr. Crisp doesn't work here anymore."

"What do you mean my father doesn't work there anymore?" I said angrily. "Let me talk to Henry."

"I'll see if Mr. Price is available. Who may I tell him is calling?"

"Luke Crisp," I said again. She put me on hold. It was a full two minutes before Henry answered. "Speaking of the devil," he said. "How are you?"

"Henry, where's my father?"

"Am I your father's keeper?"

"The receptionist said he's no longer there."

"She's my new assistant," Henry said, "and no, he's not. He retired, Luke."

I was speechless. "Retired?"

"Isn't that what you suggested? How do you not know this?"

"I haven't spoken with my father since I left."

"Then you don't know about his surgery."

"What surgery?"

"What surgery? His triple bypass."

"Wha . . . Henry, no one told me," I said.

"You broke his heart, you know. Maybe literally. I'm not surprised he hasn't been in contact with you. You let him down and you weren't there for him when he needed you. Now I understand why he said what he did."

"What did he say?"

"He told me you're dead to him."

The words hit me like a bucket of ice water. "He said that?"

"His exact words were, 'I have no son.' "

For a moment neither of us spoke.

"So what brings you back now—run out of dough?"

When I didn't answer, he said, "I thought so. Good luck, Luke. You made your bed, now sleep in it." He hung up. I slowly dropped the phone to my lap. I sat frozen, Candace staring at me. My worst fears had been confirmed.

"What did your father say?" she asked.

"My father's no longer at Crisp's." I looked down, fighting the wave of emotion that swept over me. "My father had a heart bypass."

"You need to go back to him," Candace said.

My eyes welled up. "I can't. He's disowned me."

Candace buried her head in her hands. After a few minutes I put my hand on her back to comfort her. "We've got to keep it together," I said. "Everything will be okay."

She looked up at me, her mascara running down her face. "Are you in denial? What part of this will be okay? How will we live?"

"Like the rest of the world does. We'll get jobs. We've got M.B.A.s, we'll do all right."

Candace didn't say anything. She dropped her gaze and slumped forward, hiding her face in her hands. For the next fifteen minutes Candace just sat, crying. When she finally stopped, she looked up at me. "I'm sorry. I think, with how things are, we need to rethink things."

I looked at her. "What exactly does that mean?"

"It means I'm not sure about all this."

"All this? You mean us?"

"Yes. Us."

My chest constricted with anger. "There wasn't a problem with *us* when I had money."

"Don't make me into a gold digger. Did I ask you to go to Europe? Didn't I tell you that you were spending too much?"

"Then what's the problem?" I said.

"It's *this*. Starting from scratch. I can't do it."

"We can do it together. We'll build a life together."

"And lose the best years of our lives."

"It doesn't have to be that way. These could be the best years of our lives. We'll be together."

"We'll learn to hate each other."

I couldn't believe what she was saying. "Why would you say that?"

"You have no idea. I've lived through it. I watched it my whole life. I watched my parents sacrifice and scrimp and save until it destroyed their marriage. When they finally started getting ahead, my father left. That's how it is."

"That's not how it is," I said angrily.

"You don't know." She exhaled slowly. "I love you, Luke. But I never signed up for that kind of life—clipping coupons to survive. It's not what I want. I don't know if I can or can't do it, but I know that I don't want to." She looked into my eyes. "I'm really sorry."

She got up and began packing her things while I just sat on the bed, watching her. When she finished, she walked to the doorway, then stopped. "I really am sorry, Luke. We'll talk in a few days, okay?"

I just looked at her. She walked out, closing the door behind herself. Something told me I'd never see her again.

CHAPTER

Twenty-Four

The only thing more universal to the human condition than love is loss.

✦ Luke Crisp's Diary ✦

I drank until early in the morning and slept through the rest of it, well into the next afternoon, when the room's phone rang. My head was throbbing. I answered hoping it was Candace. It was the front desk asking if I was going to check out or if they should charge me for another day. I told them that I was leaving. Without showering or changing my clothes, I grabbed my suitcase and carry-on bag and left the room.

Where would I go? I felt like a man who had just stepped over a cliff wishing to take back just a few steps. Even the $3,000 I'd spent on the cabana could have provided several months' stay in a cheap hotel. What do you do when you have no place to go? I was in a daze as I walked out of my room.

I took the elevator down to the lobby. The electricity and cash of the casino flowed around me, past me, like a river. I sat down at a bar and ate the free bar nuts and crackers and drank more and mostly just watched. Around midnight I fell asleep in the chair. The bartender woke me. "Sorry, sir, you can't sleep here."

I got up. I dragged my luggage to another part of the

casino, fighting my exhaustion. My thoughts rolled and bounced around in my head like a ball on one of the casino's roulette wheels. The world looked different to me now. Changed. I realized that I had lived my life on a different level of humanity—one where money was both ubiquitous and intangible. Most of my life I didn't even carry money, just magical plastic cards that got me whatever I needed— like a VIP pass to the world. Unlike paper money, the plastic never diminished. It did, of course, but not where one could see it.

I never checked receipts; I rarely looked at price tags. I realized that Candace was right—I didn't know want or scarcity. I had lived in a different world than most people. Now I was in their world. Actually, I was below their world. I had no job, no home and no money. There was no safety net below me. How could I have been so stupid?

I thought back to that dinner with my father when he suggested I go to business school. How ironic—he said he didn't want me to have any regrets. That's all I had now. Regret and hate. I hated Sean more that I could say. I wished that I had let the gamblers take their pound of flesh. But I hated myself even more for being taken in by him.

What weighed just as heavily on me was Candace's betrayal. I was in love with her. I thought she was in love with me. I had heard it said that men want beautiful women and women want beautiful situations. I didn't believe it at the time. I did now. Is that really all I was to Candace? A lifestyle? The thought of it was like putting my heart between the hammer and the anvil.

Here I was in a neon jungle just as helpless as if I were lost in the Amazon jungle. I took out my wallet. Worthless plastic and a little more than $500. Then I remembered Candace's ring. It had cost nearly $30,000. I just needed to find a place to sell it. I would sell it in the morning. I felt some peace again. Thirty thousand was enough of a safety net to get me through this. I put my wallet in my bag, then closed my eyes and fell asleep. It was around three o'clock in the morning when a security guard woke me.

"Sir," he said.

I looked up. "Yeah."

"Are you okay?"

"Sorry, I just fell asleep. I'll go." I slowly stood up. "Sorry."

I put my carry-on on top of my suitcase and dragged it behind me out of the casino. I felt like I was sleepwalking. Once outside the lobby, I looked around for a place to go. Despite the hour, the traffic on the street in front of the hotel was nearly as heavy as at midday. The strip stretched on for miles and I was too tired to walk. I just needed a place where I could lie down for an hour or two.

At the end of the resort's massive parking lot, there was a clump of trees. I crossed the parking lot, pulling my bags behind me. When I could see no one was looking, I entered the grove, lay my jacket out on the ground and fell asleep. I woke late the next morning to a light kick in my side.

"Stand up, sir."

I looked up to see a police officer standing above me. "I haven't been drinking," I said.

"I've heard that before," he said.

I sat up. "You can smell my breath if you want."

"Thanks, but I'll pass."

"I've been staying at the Bellagio. I just lost all my money."

"I've heard that before too. May I see your I.D., please?"

"It's in my bag." I turned to get it. My bag was gone. My suitcase was still there, but my carry-on bag had disappeared. Everything I needed was in the bag: my wallet, my I.D., my money and my cell phone. Then it hit me, the ring was gone too. I looked around frantically. "I've been robbed."

The officer just looked at me. "No I.D.?"

"I had a ring in there. It was worth thirty thousand dollars."

"I just need your I.D."

"Didn't you hear me? I've been robbed. My bag had everything!"

He looked at me dully. "Do you want to file a report?"

I wanted to scream. "Will it do any good?"

"It will for your insurance claim. Or if someone turns it in, we can contact you."

"Contact me on what? My stolen cell phone?"

"Sir, settle down."

I wanted to throttle this guy. When I had gained control, I said, "I have nothing. I have no place to go."

"There's a rescue mission up off Bonanza. They have beds and a soup kitchen." He pointed. "It's straight up the boulevard from here."

"I'm not sleeping in a homeless shelter."

"I don't care where you sleep, as long as it's not here."

I stood and wiped the dirt from my pant legs. "Eight months ago I had a million dollars," I said.

"Vegas is magic. You can see David Copperfield make an elephant disappear or go to a casino and make a fortune disappear."

"Are there any pawnshops around here?"

"That's like asking if there are any casinos." He walked back to his patrol car and sat there until I walked away.

✦

I walked up the boulevard. Pawnshops are ubiquitous in Vegas—they follow gambling like seagulls follow shrimp boats. I had never been inside a pawnshop before. It looked like an indoor flea market without the energy. The place was dirty and dank, with surveillance cameras in the corner of the room. At the back of the shop was a wooden counter and behind it were rows of guns locked up in a case. A large man wearing a Stan Ridgway T-shirt, bald with a goatee, sat behind the counter looking at me with a grim expression. "What can I do you for?" he asked in a gravelly voice.

"I've got to sell some things," I said.

"Whatcha got?"

"I've got an iPad and an iPod," I said.

"Anything else?"

"Some clothes."

"Don't do clothes."

"They're expensive clothes," I said.

"Don't do clothes," he repeated. "Let me see the electronics."

I took them out of my suitcase and set them on the counter.

"I'll give you two hundred dollars for the iPad and seventy-five for the iPod."

"How about my suitcase?"

He looked at it. "Fair condition. I'll give you forty-five dollars for it."

"Forty-five dollars? It's a Louis Vuitton. It was over three hundred dollars new."

"It's not new anymore."

"How about two hundred dollars?"

"I'll give you fifty-five. Final offer."

I looked at the bag. I wasn't about to carry it around with me. "Do you have any backpacks?"

He pointed to the wall. "Over on that shelf."

"How much are they?"

"Depends on the pack."

I walked over and selected one that was big enough to fit my clothing, but not so big to look like I was camping. I checked the price tag: $27. I looked back at him. "How about I trade you the suitcase for this pack and fifty dollars."

"What's the price on it."

"Twenty-seven dollars."

"Then I'll give you the pack and twenty-eight dollars."

The guy wasn't budging. I relented, bringing the pack up to the front. I filled it up with my clothes, then lifted my suitcase up to the counter.

"Don't put it up here," he said. "Just leave it on the floor."

"Sorry," I said, setting it back down.

He took out a calculator and a pad of paper and pen. "We got an iPad for two hundred, an iPod classic for fifty-five."

"Seventy-five," I corrected.

He looked at me. "Seventy-five. Then fifty-five for the suitcase minus twenty-seven for the pack, the total is three hundred and three." He opened his register and took out some bills. "Here's your money."

I put the money in my front pocket, then turned and walked out. I sat down on the sidewalk near the side of the building to think. I knew I wasn't thinking right. I was depressed, angry, desperate and scared. I had $303 to my name. I needed to conserve every dime until I could create some kind of situation for myself. I had to come up with a plan before what little money I had left was gone—before my clothes were dirty and I stank too much for anyone to hire me.

Hire me? How would I get a job? I had skills and schooling, but I had no I.D., no address, no résumé and no phone. I had hired dozens of people for Crisp's and I had never hired anyone on the spot. It was always a phone call the next few days or weeks. Where would they call? And even if someone did hire me immediately, it would be weeks before I received my first paycheck. How would I cash it without I.D.? I began to understand the downward spiral of homelessness.

There had to be somewhere else I could go for help, if I could just think of it. As I thought of the people I knew, the reality of my life hit me like a truncheon. I had no friends— no one I kept in regular touch with. I suppose that was part of the initial allure of the Wharton clan—it was the first group outside of a work environment that I had belonged to. I had no church. No social club. No fraternity. In college I went from class to work and then home. The only friends I had, if you can call them friends, were my associates from the copy centers, and, because I was their manager, none of those were close. At the time I blamed it on the stigma of officers fraternizing with the troops, but the truth was, I just didn't have time for anyone.

Sadly enough, the Wharton group was it. Sean and Marshall were users and Candace had left me. Suzie was who knows where. Lucy would help, if she could, but she didn't have any money and I didn't even know where she was. The only one I knew I could turn to in a crunch was James. And he was gone.

As far as family went, I was in equally bad shape. My grandparents on both sides had passed away years earlier. The only relatives I had from my mother's side lived back East, and the last time I'd seen any of them was at my mother's funeral when I was seven. The closest thing I had to a family was the group my father had created: Henry, who had thrown me to the curb, Mary, who was an appendage to my father and would do nothing without his consent, and my Aunt Barbara and Uncle Paul. I knew Barbara and Paul well enough to know that they would side with my father.

As awful as it sounded, spending the night at the homeless shelter seemed to be my best option until I got things figured out.

I spent the afternoon making my way to the rescue mission. It was easy to find. There was a massive gathering of humanity in front of the building. I felt uneasy as I approached the crowd. Some of those around me were obviously mentally ill, talking to themselves; some were shaking, addicts of one substance or another; then others were just people like me, down on their luck. People like me? I doubted there were many displaced millionaires in the crowd.

I pushed my way to the front, looking around for someone to explain how things worked when a woman shouted at me, "Get back in line!" She pointed at me and almost everyone around me turned to look at me. Drawing attention to myself was the last thing I wanted.

A large man covered in tattoos shoved me. "Get in line."

"I'm trying to find the line," I said.

A moment later a man near the shelter's door raised his hands and shouted, "That's it, that's it."

I turned to the man behind me. He wore army fatigues and his gray hair was pulled back in a ponytail. "What's he talking about?"

"They're out of room," he said.

"So what do we do?"

He looked at me with an amused expression. "Find a nice dumpster, somewhere that don't smell too much, and make sure it ain't on trash day. I lost a buddy that way."

"I'm not sleeping in a dumpster," I said.

"Suit yourself," he said. "There's always the tunnels."

"What are the tunnels?"

"Flood tunnels under the city. There's a whole world underground."

"Where do you find them?"

He grinned. "They're everywhere, pal. There's one underneath you right now. But you'll need a flashlight. And a knife."

"Why a knife?"

"You never know who's down there."

⋆

My world had transformed from dream to nightmare. *I wasn't like these people,* I told myself, *these "homeless." I had run a multimillion-dollar business. I had an M.B.A. from Wharton. I'd stayed in Napoleon's house.*

These thoughts brought me no comfort. No, I wasn't like them. I wasn't as smart. If they had that kind of money, they would cling to it like a life raft. They wouldn't have given a dime to Sean.

I walked around the area until two in the morning—until I couldn't walk anymore. I was tempted to use the money I had in my pocket for a cheap hotel room, but that would be shortsighted. What would I eat with? I found a place to sleep behind a pyracantha bush in a park. Sleep isn't the best description of what I did. I think I woke at every sound. Being homeless is a frightening thing.

Years earlier, in my college sociology class, the professor asked us to contemplate what it would be like to be dropped into a foreign country without shelter, friends or currency. I never imagined that I'd have the opportunity to find out firsthand what that would be like. Over the next few days I learned about this culture I was now a part of. I was amazed at how uncomfortable "normal" people were around me and became aware of their subtle, furtive glances of pity or disdain.

I learned that there were more than 14,000 homeless in the city and just a small number of beds available for them. Even then, many of the homeless stayed away from the shelters after being beaten up, having their things stolen or both.

The streets weren't any safer of course. The homeless fall victim to other homeless, drug addicts, gangs and sometimes even the police. In civilized society there are rules, courtesies and pretenses, but they don't apply to those on the street. The concrete outdoors is as mean a world as nature itself—a violent world, where the strong prey on the weak.

> *If you couldn't get out of the quicksand*
> *when you were strong,*
> *how are you going to get out*
> *after you've lost all your strength?*

✦ Luke Crisp's Diary ✦

For the next few days my space behind the bush at the park was my home base. I found some cardboard, which I laid flat over the bush's fallen needles. I bought a loaf of bread and a box of crackers, a package of toilet paper and a plastic bottle of water, which I purchased more for the receptacle than the liquid.

I bought a newspaper and started looking through the help wanted ads. I found a few openings for managerial positions and I called from a pay phone at a 7-Eleven to schedule interviews. My first interview was two days later with an office supply company. The day of the interview I shaved and washed myself with paper towels from the sink at a nearby gas station, then put on my cleanest clothes. As I looked at myself in the mirror, I wished that I hadn't let my hair grow so long in Europe. I did my best to make it look good, then walked four and a half miles to the interview.

I arrived at the interview sweat-stained from my walk, sunburned from exposure and puffy-eyed from lack of sleep. I had, out of necessity, brought my backpack, which looked out of place in the corporate environment.

The receptionist was indifferent toward me and I waited in the lobby for nearly an hour, which, frankly, I didn't mind, as it was air conditioned and furnished with soft, vinyl couches.

When the HR director finally walked out into the lobby to get me, I could see from her eyes that I had already failed the interview.

The first thing the woman asked was to see my résumé, which I didn't have, though I offered her a verbal one. She listened to me for a moment, but I could tell it was only out of courtesy. She asked just a few more surface questions (the obligatory kind, not the ones you ask when you're serious about hiring), then said they'd give me a call if they decided to hire me—ignoring the fact that she'd never asked for my phone number.

Over the next week I went to three more interviews, all with similar results. Actually, worse results, probably due to my increasing desperation. My father used to say, "The world only offers you what you don't need." He may have been right. You can't get a bank loan until you can prove you don't need it, and it's tough to get a job if you don't already have one.

In spite of my thrift and near starvation, I was quickly running low on money, so after just one week of rejection I decided to lower my sights and applied for four custodial positions. If I couldn't work in an office I could, in the meantime, clean one. I was astonished to find out how competitive it was to get a job cleaning a building—even a warehouse.

Actually, the interviews for the custodial positions were more painful than those for the managerial positions. One of them was with the daughter of the owner of a wholesale plumbing supply outlet. I had graduated summa cum laude from ASU, earned an M.B.A. from Wharton, had managed a multimillion-dollar business before I was twenty, and there I was in a warehouse, sitting in a taped vinyl chair at the mercy of a nineteen-year-old girl who had a lip ring, two nose rings, a massive tattoo on her neck and kept saying "we was." I didn't get the job. I didn't get any of them.

By the end of my third week on the street, I was overcome with despair. I felt like I was walking in a haze, which is no surprise since I don't think I had slept for more than two hours straight since I'd left the Bellagio.

One morning I saw my reflection in the glass window of a building and had to stop to make sure it was me. I was unshaven and dirty and my hair was long and matted to one side. I realized what people saw when I applied for a job. I looked miserable. I looked homeless.

CHAPTER

Twenty-Five

Under the Las Vegas streets resides a silent,
subterranean village of the city's homeless.
"It's not a bad life," one of the tunnel dwellers said to me.
"Two walls and a roof overhead. Beats sleeping in the park."

✦ Luke Crisp's Diary ✦

Living in the park was getting more untenable. One night I heard a drug deal going down just on the other side of the bush. Fortunately for me they didn't know I was there. Another night, I woke to the sound of a police radio. I peeked out of my space to see three patrol cars parked on the near side of the park. Someone had been stabbed to death. That's when I decided to move.

The next morning I went into a thrift store and bought a flashlight with batteries, a sleeping bag, an inflatable cushion, a package of toilet paper and a bowie knife. I strapped the knife to my leg and fastened the sleeping bag and cushion to my pack. In my walking I had passed the opening to one of the flood tunnels about a mile from the park. As I walked toward the tunnel, I felt like I was walking into the mouth of a beast—one that might swallow me forever.

I turned on my flashlight and went inside. I passed two people—one drunk, the other passed out—about twenty yards from the entry. I kept on walking through the darkness. Not counting the rats, I didn't see anyone else, though I passed several places that stank of urine or feces. About a hundred yards from the tunnel's entrance I found a place where someone had spray-painted HOME SWEET HOME.

I laid my flashlight against the concrete wall, then made a nest of some scraps lying around, cardboard and newspapers, inflated my pad and rolled out my sleeping bag. I turned off the flashlight, and lay back. Before I fell asleep, a thought went through my mind—the same thing I had thought in Saint-Tropez: *If only Dad could see me now.*

During the time I spent underground, I met scores of people, including a couple who had brought in a bed with a headboard. They also had Ansel Adams prints leaning against the tunnel's concrete wall—all the comforts of home. I don't know if the tunnels ever flooded, they didn't while I was there, but most of the time a small stream of runoff ran through the center, which we used to bathe.

✦

Some time after I'd moved into the tunnel, Christmas decorations began appearing in the store windows outside. It's strange how irrelevant time becomes when there's nothing to pin it to. I had no calendar, no watch and no reason to own either. There were no events in my life, no dates, no holidays, just daily survival. I kept telling myself that I was still going to escape, but each day it seemed less likely. I ate at the soup kitchen when I could, but not always, and my money was dwindling. The weather got colder, but not intolerable. I suppose the moderate winter is one of the reasons Vegas attracts so many homeless—at least those that it doesn't produce itself. If I was just one state north, I might have frozen to death.

As I became more depressed, I became more nocturnal, usually beginning my day around 4 P.M., eating dinner at the soup kitchen, then wandering around at night. I preferred the world at night, when it was less crowded—when normal people slept and the world was left to us, the invisible. I didn't do much but think. That's all there was to do, think and walk.

One night I was crossing through a home supply store's parking lot when I was attacked by two men. I didn't run as I didn't even see them coming. I was immediately knocked to the ground.

Looking back, what was most disturbing about the assault was the quiet, settled nature of it—two predators surrounding their prey. Their eyes held no remorse, no guilt, no mercy, just a quiet understanding that that's just the way it is in nature, red in tooth and claw. Being homeless is dehumanizing, but I think it was only then that I realized just how much of an animal I was.

Both of the men had knives. I had a knife too, but my instincts told me that to use it was certain death. I might die anyway, but maybe not. Frankly, it didn't matter a whole lot to me.

The entire incident was like an out-of-body experience— flashing about me like images in a strobe light; splatters of sweat or blood, a fist or shoe followed by a flash of pain. Yet, even in my desperation and fear, my mind continued to process. I wondered what my father would think when he learned that his only son had died homeless. Would it make the papers? The *Wall Street Journal*? It might. It was good copy—son of multimillionaire found homeless and murdered. Crisp's stock prices might even drop.

The press would likely blame my father—the public is always looking for a scapegoat—but I knew better. I had brought this on myself. I could blame Sean, the system, fate or even God, but in the end, I had been on this path from the moment I turned from my father. It was my choice. I may not have liked my destination, but I had chosen the path.

CHAPTER

Twenty-Six

*I have learned that real angels don't have
gossamer white robes and cherubic skin.
They have calloused hands and smell of the day's sweat.*

✦ Luke Crisp's Diary ✦

I was beaten unconscious. Everything was taken from me except my boxer shorts and my life, which I now regarded with equal value. I woke in a puddle of water, but not blood. My nose was bleeding, but that was it. They hadn't cut me. They hadn't killed me. My backpack was gone. The last of my money was gone. The streets had beaten me.

As I lay there, aching and gathering my senses, headlights appeared. I was exposed, curled in a fetal ball. The vehicle pulled close. My body shook from the trauma. I saw a man getting out of his van and more terror filled me. *What did he want from me? What was he going to do to me?*

The man knelt down at my side. "You okay, brother?"

I looked up at him. Through the haze of my pain and fear, I saw a Hispanic man, short and broad, probably in his mid-to-late fifties. His eyes were dark as coal, and he had a large, thick scar on his right cheek, wide, like a burn. "I'm hurt," I said.

"Do you think you can get up?"

"I don't know."

"I'll help you."

I groaned as I forced myself to my knees. He took my arm

and helped me to my feet. As I stood, a sharp pain flashed across my abdomen. "My ribs," I said. "I must have broken some ribs."

"C'mon," the man said. "Let's get out of here in case whoever did this decides to come back."

Still holding my arm, he helped me to the passenger side of the van. The van was long and white, with windows running down its length. There was printing on the outside of the van, but I didn't read it. The man opened the door for me. "Can you get in?"

"I'll try," I said.

Climbing into the van was intensely painful, but I managed to get in and sit back, my hands crossed at my chest. He shut my door, then walked around the front and climbed into the driver's seat, locked the doors and started the van. He quickly backed up, then pulled out onto the boulevard. "You're still bleeding," he said. "From your nose."

I wiped my nose with my forearm. "Sorry."

He reached down on the floor next to him and lifted a rag that was between the seats. "It's a little dirty, but you can wipe the blood off with it."

"Thanks." I wiped my face with the cloth, which turned dark with blood and dirt. When we'd gone a block, the man said, "I'm Carlos Sanchez."

"Carlos," I said. "Thank you."

"Don't mention it. What's your name?"

"Luke."

"Should I take you to the hospital? There's one a half mile from here."

"No," I said. "I'll be all right." The idea of sitting in the waiting room in my underwear was more than I could handle. Also, I didn't have any money. I doubted that they could legally turn me away, but the composite humiliation of the experience seemed nearly as bad as my beating. I doubted that they could do anything anyway.

"You sure?"

"Yeah. They can't fix ribs."

"You may be hurt worse than you know. You could have internal bleeding."

"I don't care," I said.

Carlos didn't know how to respond to that. After a moment he said, "Where should I take you?"

"It doesn't matter," I said.

"You're homeless?"

"Yes." I breathed out heavily. "You wouldn't happen to have a spare set of clothes in here would you?" I asked flippantly.

"Just what I got on." After a moment he said, "There's a shelter over off Bonanza. They probably have some clothes and stuff."

"They won't help tonight. You have to be there early to get in."

He looked vexed again. I figured he was trying to decide what to do with me.

"Do you have anything to eat?" I asked.

"No," he said. "But we can stop and get something."

"I'd appreciate that," I said.

"No problem." He reached down and turned on the radio.

Classic rock. A Guess Who song was playing, "Bus Rider." My father used to listen to them ad nauseum. "Real rock," he called it.

After we'd gone a bit farther, I asked, "Why did you stop?"

He turned and looked at me as if I'd asked a dumb question. "You needed help."

"Thank you," I said again.

"There's an In-N-Out Burger up ahead," Carlos said. "That okay?"

"I'm not picky."

"I was going to stop for a burger anyway." A moment later he pulled into the driveway of the restaurant, stopping at its posted menu. "What do you want?"

"I'll eat anything."

"I'll get you what I'm getting." He turned down the radio and drove up to the restaurant's speaker box. A nasal voice came over the intercom. "Welcome to In-N-Out Burger. What may we get for you?"

"Two large cheeseburgers with fries and Coke . . ." He looked at me: "Coke?"

I nodded.

". . . And two strawberry shakes," he said.

My mouth watered.

"Pull ahead to the first window," the voice squawked.

Carlos drove his van forward. The woman inside said, "That'll be ten seventy-three." Carlos thumbed through his wallet, handing the woman a couple bills.

"Sorry, I don't have any money," I said.

"Brother, you don't even have a pocket to put money in."

He looked at me and smiled. I grinned. I thought he was the coolest man in the world.

The woman inside the drive-thru window gave Carlos his change and then looked over at me. I'm sure she was wondering what I was doing in my boxers. Then again, maybe not. We were in Vegas. Anything goes in Vegas.

We got our food, and Carlos pulled ahead into a parking space and killed the van. I hadn't had anything to eat for almost twenty-four hours and I wolfed down the food.

He watched me eat with amusement. "Good, huh?"

"Manna," I said. "Thank you."

"You're welcome."

I finished the burger, then started in on my shake. "What do you do for a living?" I asked.

"I'm the administrator of the Golden Age Senior Care Center."

"Is that like a convalescent center?"

"Yes. But the industry doesn't use that term anymore." He glanced over. "Conjures up images of old people waiting to die."

I nodded. "You're right. Care Center sounds better."

We both kept eating. "Where are you from?" Carlos asked.

"Phoenix."

"I like Phoenix," he said. "I was there for an elderly care conference a couple months ago. Stayed at this ritzy place— the Camelback Inn." He took another bite of his burger. "It was really nice."

"In Scottsdale," I said.

"Right. We played some golf there."

"The Padre or the Indian Bend course?"

"Indian Bend." He looked at me with a peculiar expression. "You've golfed there?"

"I was a member of the resort's golf club."

Carlos took a few more bites of his food then said, "You're not the typical homeless guy. At least not like any I've ever met."

"What do you mean?"

"You had a golf club membership. You're well spoken. Did you go to college?"

"Yeah. I got my undergraduate at ASU. My M.B.A. at Wharton."

"You went to Wharton? That's an Ivy League school," he said. "I was right, you're not like everyone else."

I could tell that the incongruency of my situation bothered him. He took a few more bites. "Wharton, huh? Bet that cost a pretty one."

"Fortune," I said. "I'm a riches-to-rags story in the flesh."

He nodded as if he suddenly understood. "Gambling?"

"No. I just got in with the wrong crowd."

"That happens too," he said. He took a long drink of his Coke, then asked, "How are you feeling?"

"Mostly my face and my ribs hurt."

"Broken ribs hurt," Carlos said, nodding. "When I was twenty, I was body surfing in Baja and got caught by a wave. They call it maytagging down there—getting thrown around in the washing machine. Broke five ribs. Hurt like the devil. Just don't cough or laugh."

"I won't be laughing much," I said. "But I can't guarantee the former."

Carlos finished his burger, then started on his fries as I noisily finished my shake. He smiled at the sound of my slurping. "Are you still hungry?" he asked.

"A little."

"Just a minute. I'll be right back." He climbed out of the van. I noticed he left the keys in the ignition. He was gone a while, nearly ten minutes. He returned with another sack and a cup with a straw protruding. He opened the door and handed me the drink, then climbed in himself. "Sorry that took so long. You wouldn't expect that long of a wait this late."

"No problem," I said.

"I got you another cheeseburger and another shake. You looked like you were really enjoying that shake."

"Thanks," I said. "I was."

Talk about the theory of relativity—I was enjoying this food every bit as much as any of our gourmet meals in New York or France. Probably more so.

"You know you left the keys in the ignition," I said.

"I don't figure a man who went to Wharton and had a golf membership at the Camelback Inn would steal an ugly van."

I grinned. "Guess not."

He looked at me for a moment and then said, "When was the last time you worked?"

"Not since I left for business school. But before that I worked since I was twelve. My father taught me to work. To him hard work was the eleventh commandment."

"Maybe we can help each other out," Carlos said. "We had four employees leave without notice last week, actually, two of them were deported, so we're busier than a one-handed blackjack dealer. Then today one of my CNAs threatened to quit if she doesn't get some help pronto." He looked at me. "See where I'm going with this?"

"What's the deal?"

"We've got nine empty rooms at the center. You can sleep there, eat there, just work the swing shift until we can get some help in."

The offer of food and shelter filled me with relief. "I don't have any experience with that kind of work," I said, "but I'm willing to do whatever you need. I'm a quick study."

"It's not rocket science," Carlos said. "You'll be helping the CNAs feed the residents."

"Feed them?" I asked. "Like spoon-feed them?"

"Some of them require that. But most of them you'll just be wheeling down to the dining room."

"I don't have any clothes," I said, even though it was kind of obvious.

"I'll get you some CNA scrubs. You'll fit right in."

"Scrubs," I said. "Like doctors wear."

"Exactly. Clothes, clean bed, three hot meals, a hot shower, soap, shampoo, even razors."

In my previous life the offer would have sounded ridiculous. But this wasn't my previous life, it was my new reality, and it was a whole lot better than living in a concrete tunnel scavenging for food. "Sounds like a deal," I said.

"You didn't ask what the pay was."

"I thought that was the pay," I said.

"No, you'll get paid. But not much. Minimum wage."

"Minimum wage," I said. "I'll take it."

CHAPTER

Twenty-Seven

I got a job today for $8.25 an hour.
I did the math.
Even if no taxes were taken out,
I'd still have to work 58,104 hours to make as much as
I'd blown through in my forty-one-day spree.

✦ Luke Crisp's Diary ✦

The Golden Age retirement center was a small, run-down care facility. My immediate impression was that it was a place for those who couldn't afford better. Carlos pulled the van into the back parking lot and turned off the ignition. "I'm going to go inside and get you a CNA uniform. What size do you wear in pants?"

"Thirty-three waist."

"Okay." He looked me over. "And an XL top. I'll be right back."

He returned fifteen minutes later carrying a bundle of clothing with a pair of white slippers on top. He opened the van's door. "Sorry that took so long. I didn't forget about you. We had a problem with one of our residents."

"No worries," I said. "I don't have any pressing engagements."

He put the clothes on the driver's seat next to me. "Try these on."

I was still aching from my beating so it hurt a little as I pulled on the purple cotton scrubs. The pants were baggy on me. I had lost more weight than I realized. I was glad to be clothed again.

"Try the slippers," he said.

I put on the shoes. They were a little wide but otherwise fit. "They're fine," I said.

"I've got other sizes," he said. "Come inside."

Inside, the center was decorated for Christmas with a fake tree in the lobby strung with tinsel and foil garlands and Christmas lights. I thought it a shame that the tree wasn't real, as the place was pungent with geriatric smells and a little pine would have done some good.

We walked past the nurses' station to the end of the hall near the back exit. Carlos pushed open the door to the last room. There was a small bed with a nightstand and a glowing lamp next to it. "You can take this room," he said. "There's a hygiene kit in the bathroom you can use. It has razors, shaving cream, shampoo, a comb, and deodorant."

"Thank you."

"The morning shift manager comes in around seven-thirty, so I'll leave her a note so she doesn't call security on you. The kitchen starts serving at seven, so you can go down to the cafeteria and get a hot breakfast. The dining room is this way." He led me down the hall to an open room with a bright linoleum floor and small, round tables. "There you go. Any questions?" he asked.

"No. Pretty straightforward."

Carlos led me back to my room. When we got there, he said, "If you need anything, just call. Everyone here has my number. I'll be in before your shift, so I'll introduce you to Sylvia. She's the CNA on this wing. You'll be assisting her."

"Sylvia," I said. "What's a CNA?"

"Certified nursing assistant. They're the front line with the residents." He looked at me and said, "You feeling okay?"

"I'm okay," I said.

"Then I'm out of here."

"I don't know how to thank you."

"Just do a good job for the people here."

I shut the door after him, then took off my clothes and took an hour-long shower. I sat on the floor of the shower and let the warm water just run over me, washing the city off of me. I shaved, which took two razors and about twenty minutes. When I was done, I got up and washed my briefs in the shower and hung them up to dry, then put my scrubs back on. I lay down in the soft clean bed and felt human again.

CHAPTER

Twenty-Eight

*I have learned that if you have something to eat,
a roof overhead and clean water,
you should be most grateful—
you number among the world's most blessed.*

✦ Luke Crisp's Diary ✦

Light was coming in through the window blinds when I woke to the sound of yelling. I wiped the sleep from my eyes and leaned forward, momentarily forgetting that I'd been injured. The pain in my ribs quickly reminded me, taking my breath away. I waited for the pain to subside and then slid my feet over the side of the bed and put on my slippers. I stood and walked to the door and peeked out. An old man was standing in the middle of the hallway about thirty feet from me. He was brandishing a fork at the nurse, periodically thrusting it at her. "You stay away from me, you demon."

"Mr. Brown, I'm not going to hurt you."

"I'm going to hurt *you*," he said. "Don't touch me." He took a step toward her.

"Marsha!" she shouted down the hall. I couldn't see anyone around except an old woman pushing herself toward them with a walker. "Mr. Brown, put down the fork before you hurt someone."

"Who are you?" he said. "What do you want with me?"

"Mr. Brown, I'm Tammy. You know me. I take care of you."

"I don't know you. Keep away from me or I'll hurt you," he said. He took another step toward her. In spite of my pain, I quickly snuck up behind the man and locked my arms around him, firmly pinning his arms to his side. He dropped the fork as he yelled out, "Aaaagh! Police! Call the police! Call a priest! Call a priest!"

The woman sighed with relief. "Thank you. Let's get him to his room and get him his medication." She brought over a wheelchair and I helped Mr. Brown into it, then she wheeled him back to his room. After Mr. Brown had calmed down, she said to me, "I owe you. What's your name?"

"I'm Luke."

"Tammy," she said, extending her hand. "You're the new guy—the one who lives here."

"That's me."

"Well, I'm glad you were here. Mr. Brown might have skewered me."

"I'm glad I was here too," I said. "Do you have any Advil or Tylenol?"

"We've got every painkiller in the book." She suddenly looked worried. "Did Mr. Brown hurt you?"

"No. I took a fall last night."

"I'll get you something." She walked away, returning a moment later with a small plastic cup with a single pill in it and a cup of water. "Eight hundred milligrams of Tylenol. I can get you something stronger when the doctor gets here."

"Thank you."

"Don't mention it," she said. "I need to check on the residents. You're working the swing shift, right?"

"That's what Carlos said."

"Well, I hope it works out," she said, then went back to work.

✦

About an hour later I went down to the dining room to get some breakfast. As I sat down at a table, an old man waddled up to me. He had dark eyes, a frown that seemed carved into his wrinkled face and gray hair that stood up on both sides like horns, or a deranged Bozo the Clown, "What are you doin' here?" he demanded.

"Getting some breakfast," I said.

"Who are you?"

I instinctively extended my hand. "I'm Luke."

He made no effort to take my hand. "I don't know any Lukes. Get out of here. Quit eating our food."

"I work here."

"I've never seen you before. You're a freeloadin' carpetbagger. Get out before I throw you out."

I just looked at him. Even though he was about half my size, I had no doubt that he might at least try to do what he threatened. I wasn't sure what to do. Taking down one of the residents probably wasn't the best way to start my first day at work.

"Why don't you just let me eat," I said.

"I'm warning you," he said, raising a feeble fist. "Pow."

As I was considering my options, another resident, a big man with a white beard and pushing a walker, stepped up to my table. He looked like a department store Santa Claus. "Calm down, Harold. He works here."

"You don't know nuthin', you North Pole reject. He looks like a scoundrel. Look at those beady eyes. He'll rob us blind in our sleep."

Santa winked at me. "No, no, no . . ." I'm not sure if it was on purpose, but he said this sounding a little like Ho, Ho, Ho. ". . . He's a good guy. He works here."

"You don't know nuthin'."

"I know that they're going to run out of cheese Danishes."

"What?" Harold turned back toward the kitchen windows, then waddled off toward them.

"Nice move," I said.

"I know a few tricks," the man said. He reached out his hand. "I'm David. But everyone here just calls me Nick."

I cocked my head. "Nick?"

"I look like St. Nicholas," he said.

I grinned. "Thanks for stepping in."

"Harold's a bit tough on the newbies. But he's not a bad guy once you get to know him. Just a bit ornery."

"I didn't notice," I said.

He laughed deeply, a Santa laugh, then patted my shoulder. "I hope you like it here." Then he slowly walked away.

One of the servers walked up to me. She was a Vietnamese woman wearing a hairnet. "Hi. What can I get you?"

"Just give me everything," I said.

"Everything," she said. "How would you like it?"

"What do you mean?"

"Normal, soft or puréed."

"Normal, please."

"Normal," she said, and walked away.

The breakfast seemed like a feast. Biscuits with sawmill gravy, orange juice, toast with butter, scrambled eggs and bacon. I finished my plate and went back to the kitchen for seconds. When I finished eating, I went to the nurses' station and found Tammy. She was reviewing a patient's chart.

"I just met one of your residents," I said. "He doesn't like me."

"Let me guess—Harold."

"How'd you guess?"

"Harold Mantilla. Most of the residents call him the Hun. He's a bit crochety. I just keep my distance. Easier that way."

"I'll consider myself warned."

Carlos arrived at the center around noon. I was lying on my bed watching television when he knocked on my door. I got up and opened the door for him.

"Good morning," he said. "I understand that you've already made yourself useful."

"You must be referring to the Mr. Brown fork incident."

"It gets exciting around here sometimes." He noticed my underwear hanging from the bathroom door handle. "We have a washing facility," he said. "Just put what needs to be washed in that laundry bag and they'll return it before dinner."

"Better service than the Château de la Messardière," I said.

"I'll take your word for it. Have you had lunch?"

"No."

"Let's get you something. I need to get some employment information on you and I'll introduce you to Sylvia."

"Does she know I'm coming?"

"Yes. And she's very, very happy."

We walked out of my room to the nurses' station. A twenty-something-year-old woman, with dark hair and a narrow face, smiled as we approached. "Sylvia," Carlos said, "this is Luke."

She smiled warmly. "Glad to meet you, Luke."

"I told Luke that he would mostly be working with serving meals."

"Perfect," she said.

"We're going to get some lunch, then I want him to see Dr. Kuo. Afterward he's all yours."

"I'll be waiting."

✦

Carlos and I ate lunch, then went back to his office to fill out my employment paperwork. We had only been there a few minutes when a man knocked on the door, then stepped inside. He was Asian, dressed casually in corduroy jeans and a flannel shirt. He had a stethoscope around his neck.

"Sorry that took so long," he said. "Mrs. Mather had a lot on her mind today."

"No problem," Carlos said, "we just finished lunch. Luke, this is Dr. Kuo. He's our resident physician."

"Nice to meet you," I said.

"Likewise," he said, shaking my hand. "Carlos told me that you got mugged last night."

"Yeah. I think they broke some ribs."

"Let's go see."

I followed the doctor to his office halfway down the east hallway. Once we were inside, he shut the door and said, "Take off your shirt, please."

I took it off, folding it over the back of a chair. My body had dark, purple bruises all over.

"They left a few marks," he said. "Any place hurt in particular?"

"Mostly the right side."

He gently ran his fingers up my ribs. "Are you having any trouble breathing?"

"No. But it hurts when I cough."

He placed his stethoscope on my back. "What we worry about is a punctured lung. Try to take a deep breath, if you can."

I breathed in slowly.

He moved the stethoscope to my other side, listened, then removed it. "Your lungs sound fine. You probably just bruised your ribs. It will take a few weeks to heal, but you'll be okay. You can get dressed."

I put my shirt back on.

"Are you on any medications?"

"No."

"Allergic to anything?"

"Not that I know of."

He wrote out a prescription. "They can fill this here. Just

ask one of the nurses. I've prescribed Tylenol Three with codeine. You probably can get by with just regular Tylenol during the day, but this will help at night."

"Thanks."

"Don't mention it. If the pain gets worse or you have trouble breathing, I'm always on call."

"Thank you," I said again. It felt good to say it. It felt good to feel truly grateful. I had learned a great truth: Joy isn't the natural response to blessings—joy is what comes from acknowledging them.

CHAPTER

Twenty-Nine

Helping others carries its own rewards—the first of which is a return to humanity.

✦ Luke Crisp's Diary ✦

I went back to Carlos's office, filled out my job application and tax forms, then reported to Sylvia for work.

"What did Carlos tell you about the job?" she asked.

"Not much. He said I'd mostly be helping with the meals."

"Exacto," she said. "Tammy told me you met Harold."

I nodded. "The Hun."

Sylvia frowned. "I don't like that they call him that. He's not a bad guy. He has pancreatitis so he's always in pain. Pain will make anyone cranky."

"I didn't mean to be offensive," I said.

"I think what's even more painful to him is that his son doesn't visit him. He only lives a couple miles from here. I just don't know how these people neglect their parents. You'll see it at Christmas. You'll see some of these residents sitting around waiting for family who will never come. Whatever happened to honor thy father and mother?"

I didn't say anything but felt a pang of guilt.

"Anyway, Harold's in our wing, so you'll be helping him. He usually just stays in his room."

"They can choose to do that?"

"Yes, they can do what they want. They're adults. This is a residents' rights facility. We honor the residents' wishes. So, here's the dealio. We have fifty-four beds, with an average seventy percent occupancy rate."

"About thirty-eight residents," I said.

"Yeah," she said, "So you're good with math. We actually have forty-one right now. You and I have the west wing with twenty-two residents. Our meal times are seven-fifteen to eight-fifteen, lunch is twelve-fifteen to one-fifteen and dinner is five-fifteen to six-fifteen. Usually about ten of our residents eat in their rooms, the rest we bring out to the dining room.

"Most of the residents have special dietary needs. The kitchen has their meal orders. I'll show you how it works."

I followed her to the dining room, then back into the kitchen, where three women in hairnets were busy preparing the evening's meal. Once inside the kitchen, Sylvia lifted a slip of paper from the metal food preparation counter. "The kitchen manager prints off a ticket for each resident and gives it to the kitchen, and they prepare the meals according to this slip.

"After you've brought the residents to the dining room, you deliver the meals to those who stay in their rooms. It's important that you compare the meal to this slip to make sure they match." She handed me the piece of paper. The slip had the resident's name, room and bed number.

"You'll notice this sheet says where the meal is to be served." She pointed to a place on the slip that read

DININGROOMTBL9. "That means that this resident eats in the dining room at table nine. This right here says what kind of beverage they can have."

"What's this Diet Cons?"

"Diet consistency. Some of the residents can't chew normal food so we have regular, soft mechanical and puréed. Say they had ham for lunch—regular would be the way you or I would have it, soft mechanical means it would be ground up or cut up in tiny bite-sized pieces. Puréed means . . ."

"Mush," I said.

"Exactly. Like baby food."

"What's this RCS?"

"Restricted concentrated sugar," Sylvia said. "It means she's diabetic."

"What time do we begin?"

"We start taking residents into the dining room on the hour. The state requires that residents may not be brought in more than a half hour early. I guess in the old days, some facilities would park the residents in front of their tables a couple hours before their meals. Cruel, but it saved money on staff.

"So, after you've helped the residents to the dining room, you'll deliver meals to those who stay in their rooms.

"Then you come back to the dining room and assist me in feeding the residents or whatever. After they've eaten and we've taken everyone back to their rooms, you pick up the plates in the rooms and take them to the kitchen."

"You were doing this all yourself?" I asked.

"And watching medications, bathing and dressing the residents and a thousand other things."

"You're amazing," I said. "What do I do if someone doesn't want what's on the menu?"

"The residents can choose something different if they want. They can have a chef salad, soup and sandwich, or a fruit plate. We have one resident, Mr. Bills in 16, who eats peanut butter and jelly sandwiches every night. I've even picked up a meal for residents at the In-N-Out Burger."

We walked back to the nurses' station. "Is it true you're living here at the facility?" she asked.

"Room 11," I said.

"That's different," she said, then added, "At least I don't have to worry about you showing up for work."

I helped Sylvia with a myriad of errands until a few minutes before five, when I started wheeling residents into the dining room. The process was slower than I thought it would be, and I realized that the profession required an immense amount of patience. It was a different world from the copy industry, where everything was measured in speed and deadlines.

I delivered the meals to the rooms, including Harold's, who had either forgotten that he didn't like me or had changed his mind about me. I asked him why he didn't eat his meal in the dining room. He replied, "I'm not eating with all those old people. It grosses me out."

Several of the residents were very interested in me and thanked me profusely for my help. One said to me, "You're very kind. Your mother did a good job with you."

"My father did," I said.

At 10 P.M. I said goodnight to Sylvia and clocked out. I got myself a soda and a piece of apple pie from the kitchen and took it to my room and lay back on my bed. I felt remarkably grateful. More than that, I felt like myself again. *How strange*, I thought. I wasn't just happier than I had been on the streets—I think I was happier than I was in Europe.

CHAPTER

Thirty

The truest indication of gratitude
is to return what you're grateful for.

✦ Luke Crisp's Diary ✦

A few days later Carlos called me to his office. As I walked in, he asked, "Did they teach you anything about marketing at Wharton?"

"Yes," I said. "And I used to handle the marketing for twelve of my father's stores. I'm actually pretty good at it."

"Maybe you could help me out. We've got too many open beds."

"I could help you with that," I said. "But then I'd be pushing myself out of a room."

"You get these beds filled, I'll find you a place," he said. "In fact, I'll pay you a five-hundred-dollar commission on every new contract. Fair enough?"

Thirteen beds at $500 each. "Sounds great," I said.

He looked at me thoughtfully. "I was thinking, maybe you'd like to work here permanently."

I smiled. "I appreciate the offer, but someday I'd like to make more than minimum wage."

He started laughing. "Yeah, I don't think you'd be happy even with my salary. Can't blame me for trying."

"I'll stay here as long as you need me. Besides, I have to. I don't have any clothes."

"I was thinking about that. I can advance you a little. If you like, Saturday morning I'll drive you somewhere to buy clothes."

"That would be really great." I looked at him quietly. "Carlos, why are you so good to me?"

"I told you, amigo. We're brothers, right?"

"I know," I said. "But really, why?"

He looked at me for a while, then a sad smile crossed his face. "Truth?"

"Of course."

"I understand a little about what you're going through. I'm an alcoholic. Eighteen years ago I lost my job—I almost lost my wife and children. If I'd kept it up, I probably would have lost my life. Then someone rescued me. He cleaned me up, stayed with me as I sobered up, drove me to my AA meetings and sat through every one of them with me for more than a year. He was there until I was strong enough to carry myself. I'm forever indebted to him."

"Who was he?" I asked.

"My father." Carlos's eyes started to well up. "Even good people make bad choices now and then. Everyone needs help sometimes."

I looked at him with a new understanding. "I have that kind of father too. He was always looking out for others." I shook my head. "I actually criticized him for caring too much. Whenever my father was making a big decision, he would ask, 'How will it affect the employees?' "

"What kind of business does your father have?"

"Copy centers."

"Copy centers, huh? There's a Crisp's copy center a couple blocks down." Suddenly he made the connection. "Your last name is Crisp. Your father doesn't . . ."

I nodded.

"Holy cow. What were you doing on the street?"

"It's a long story," I said. "And I better get back to work. Harold's going to be angry if I'm late."

"Come see me when you're done," he said. "We'll talk advertising."

"It's a deal, amigo."

CHAPTER

Thirty-One

I was given the chance to help Carlos.
It felt wonderful to be on the giving end for a change.

✦ Luke Crisp's Diary ✦

After I finished helping the residents with dinner, I returned to Carlos's office to discuss marketing ideas.

"We run at a thirty percent vacancy," he said, "The national norm is about thirteen. I'm doing something wrong."

"How competitive is the care center business?"

"Cutthroat," he said, running a finger across his throat. "Cutthroat."

"What kind of advertising are you currently doing?"

"I run ads in some of the local retirement publications."

"Can I see them?"

"Sure." He went to a cupboard and brought out some magazines. All of the Golden Age advertisements were marked in the magazines with Post-it notes. I looked at the ads. They were poorly written and amateurishly designed. I looked over the magazines. "These magazines are geared towards wealthy people."

"Yeah."

"Let me ask you something. If the Golden Age were a hotel, would it be a five-star? Four-star?"

"I've never thought of it that way," he said. "Most of our residents don't have a lot of money."

"Then you're in the wrong venue. It's like you're trying to sell Hyundais to people who only drive Rolls-Royces. Do you have a pad of paper?"

"Right here," he said. He handed me the paper with a pen with the center's name on it. "That's some of the advertising we do as well," he said. "We had these pens printed."

I clicked the pen open. "Tell me, why would someone stay at your place instead of your competition?"

"We're cheaper than most of them."

I wrote this down. "Anything else?"

"Our staff is nice. We don't have a lot of the frills like the more expensive places, but we're careful about who we hire. We do special personality tests."

"You didn't with me."

"I did my own version."

"So you're less expensive and you have better employees. What's your advertising budget?"

"About a thousand dollars a month."

I thought about it. "Where did you get these residents you have now?"

"I don't know."

I scribbled on the pad. "We need to find that out. I can make up a survey for you. Who usually makes the final decision to come here, the resident or someone else?"

"Usually the resident's family. Their adult children."

"Who, I'm guessing, want what's best for their parents but—and they'll never admit this—don't want to see their inheritance gobbled up either. We're onto something. What's the average age your resident comes in?"

"Late seventies."

"Then their children are probably in their fifties, late forties?"

He nodded.

I thought for a few minutes, then scribbled something on a piece of paper. When I was done, I handed the pad to Carlos. "I think we should run something like this in the local newspaper."

He looked at what I'd written:

> *Trying to decide how to care*
> *for the parents who cared for you isn't easy.*
> *You want them treated with dignity, respect and kindness.*
> *Money can't buy those things, so we don't charge for it.*
> *Exceptional care, reasonably priced.*
> *You could spend more, but you won't find better care.*
> *Golden Age.*
> *Let us care for those you care about.*

Carlos looked up. "Hey, that's good."

"Do you have someone who could put the ad together?" I asked. "A graphic artist."

"I usually do it."

I was glad I hadn't said anything derogatory about the ads he'd shown me. "Why don't I take a stab at it," I said. "Then we'll run it in the local newspaper community section."

"Okay," he said, looking excited. "We'll run it up the ol' flagpole and see if anyone salutes."

Thirty-Two

"How many hired servants of my father's
have bread enough and to spare?"
That's what the Bible asks.
I figured out a way to get more bread.

✦ Luke Crisp's Diary ✦

Saturday morning Carlos and his wife, Carmen, drove me to Henderson to buy some clothes. It was a little weird leaving the facility still dressed in my scrubs, but people just thought I was a doctor and treated me with respect. Clothes don't make the man, but they certainly make his image.

When Carmen asked me where I wanted to go shopping for clothes, I told her the places I used to go, not thinking through the fact that, on my new income, I wouldn't be able to afford anything at those stores. She just thought I was kidding.

We ended up going to a nearby Target. I bought some Levi's, khakis, loafers, a new pair of tennis shoes and a few polo shirts, spending only half of the advance that Carlos had given me.

I was overjoyed to wear normal clothes again. I had Sunday off and, for the first time since I'd come off the streets, I went out for a walk. At the first intersection away from the center, I ran into a homeless man panhandling. I gave him a $10 bill and told him where in the tunnel he could find my sleeping bag and air cushion.

I kept on walking. About three blocks from the care center I stopped at an In-N-Out Burger for a cheeseburger and a strawberry shake. As I was eating, I looked out the front window. Across the parking lot was a Crisp's copy center. I noticed that there was a DAY SHIFT, HELP WANTED sign in the window.

At that moment I knew exactly what I needed to do—the employees at Crisp's got paid well, received health and dental insurance just a month after they started and had a chance to grow a real career. It was no accident that Crisp's had made the *Top 100 American Companies to Work For* list for the last ten years. My father saw to that.

I mused over the idea. Could it be possible to get a job at Crisp's without anyone in corporate finding out? Of course it was. Even my father, who could name just about every one of the 2,000+ cities we had a center in, couldn't tell you the managers' names. Who can remember two thousand names? As an employee, I would be lost in the sea of Crisp's employees.

I finished my shake, then walked across the parking lot to the copy center. I pulled open the glass door and stepped inside, welcomed by the familiar smell of ink and paper and the light hum of copy machines. To me the sound of the machines had the same impact as a lullaby. I suddenly felt emotional. Walking into the center was like coming home.

A portly young man with acne smiled at me from the counter. He looked like he was maybe eighteen or nineteen. "May I help you?"

"I'm looking for the manager," I said.

"That would be Wayne. He won't be in until the morning."

"Thanks," I said. "I'll come back."

I lingered a moment inside the shop before I walked back to the care center.

✦

The next morning I got up at seven, put on my new street clothes, ate breakfast and returned to Crisp's. The same young man I had seen the day before greeted me. "You're back," he said.

"And you're still here. Don't they let you go home?"

He grinned. "I was putting in some overtime."

"Is your manager in?"

"Yes. May I tell him what this is regarding?"

"I saw your help wanted sign. I want to apply for a job."

"Cool. I'll get him."

A moment later a man emerged from the back office. He looked to be in his late fifties or early sixties. He had thick-rimmed glasses and white hair. If he were dressed in lederhosen, he'd be a dead ringer for Gepetto. I instinctively glanced at his name tag as he walked up to me. The name tags were the same in every Crisp's—I had helped approve the design myself four years earlier. WAYNE.

"Wayne Luna," the man said, "Like the moon. May I help you?"

I looked him in the eye. For the first time in a long time, I felt strong. This was my element. "Hello, Wayne. My name is Luke. I'd like to talk to you about the job you have posted."

He looked me over. "Okay, come on back to my office."

I followed him, stepping inside the office behind him. He sat down behind his desk. "Have a seat."

"Thank you."

"Do you have any experience working in a copy center?"

"Actually, I do. In fact, I know how to operate every machine in here."

He folded his arms across his chest, and I couldn't tell if he was impressed or skeptical. "Really?"

"Four years ago I managed a copy center in Phoenix."

"That's where our national headquarters is. What copy center did you work for?"

I looked at him, unsure how to answer. "Probably nothing you've heard of," I said. "It was just a little mom-and-pop store."

"How long did you work there?"

"About eight years. Up until I went to college. I was the manager for six years."

"Six years," he said. "How old were you when you started, fourteen?"

"Close. I was kind of a copy center prodigy."

He laughed. "All right, I'll take your word for it. Do you have a résumé?"

"No. But if you like, I could put one together on Crisp's state-of-the-art résumé preparation software."

He grinned. "That's okay. You mentioned you have some college?"

"I have a bachelors from ASU and an M.B.A."

"An M.B.A.? From where?"

I probably shouldn't have shared this detail. "Wharton."

His brow fell. "Wharton? I think you're probably over-qualified for this job."

I nodded slowly. "You know, Wayne, I've never under-stood that phrase. Why wouldn't you want someone to be overqualified? If I needed heart surgery, I'd look for a surgeon who was overqualified."

He chuckled. "Well, that's true. But this isn't a hospital and people who are overqualified don't stay put very long."

"True," I said. "But in my case, you don't have to worry. I'm not looking for something else. I love this business. I always have."

He nodded. "Your name is Luke?"

"Yes."

"Last name?"

"Crisp. Just like your copy center."

"That's peculiar. You're from Arizona, you have the same last name as our founder and you managed a copy center for six years." He raised an eyebrow. "You sure you're not some relation?"

"Would I be asking you for a job if I was?"

He smiled. "Probably not. So where do you live now?"

"I live just about three blocks from here, on the corner of Ann Road, just west of 95."

I could see him thinking. "I can't think of any apartments over there. There's just that chiropractic office and a conva-lescent home."

"Care center," I instinctively corrected. "It's near there." I looked him in the eyes. "Look, I'll make you a deal, Wayne.

Hire me for one week. If you're not completely satisfied, I'm gone. You don't even have to pay me for my time."

He crossed his arms at his chest. "Why would you do that?"

"At the risk of sounding insufferably cocky, it's because I know I'm what you're looking for. I just need the chance to prove it to you."

He considered my offer. "You didn't ask how much we pay."

"I already know," I said without thinking.

"How would you know that?"

I had to think of something fast. ". . . Because our copy center kept losing employees to Crisp's. So I knew they paid better than we did."

"That makes sense," he said. "Well, it's ten an hour to start. After thirty days we do a follow-up interview. If you're doing well, we increase it to twelve. At your six-month review it may be raised as high as fifteen. But what Crisp's is really known for is our benefits. We have an excellent retirement plan for our vested employees, and top-shelf health and dental insurance available after your thirty-day review."

"What's the ceiling at this location?"

"The manager position—my job—which I won't be giving up for a couple years."

"You have plans to leave?"

"I'm just two years away from my retirement. Like I said, Crisp's has a great pension plan, so I'm looking forward to it."

Crisp's retirement plan was among the best in the office

service industry. I used to wonder why my father wasted so much money on it, assuming it was just because he was such a nice guy. Now I realized that there was method behind his madness—he had created "golden handcuffs" to keep his best employees. My father knew what he was doing.

"So," Wayne continued, "I'm not going anywhere for a while, but we have an assistant manager for each shift and I'm about to lose my day shift manager."

"Is that a position you're looking to fill?" I asked.

"Actually, I am. Crisp's policy is to promote internally, but there are exceptions. In this case, it's a distinct possibility, since my employee with the most seniority isn't looking like managerial material." He looked at me for a moment, then said, "You really know how to run everything here? You're not just pulling my leg?"

"If I was, you'd find me out in about two minutes."

He still looked at me as if he wasn't convinced. I turned around in my chair and looked outside the office. I pointed to the nearest machine. "That's a Xerox 4110, a black and white copier with a print capacity of a hundred double-sided pages a minute. It's a great machine and the industry workhorse. You have two of them, your second one is fitted with a finisher which, from here, looks like it has saddle-stitch capability with the new box fold. I'm guessing you're operating under the standard Xerox maintenance contract."

He looked at me and grinned. "Okay. You know what you're talking about."

"Do I have the job?"

He smiled at my directness. "I don't see any reason I

wouldn't hire you. It's not every day you have a copy center prodigy walk through your door."

I grinned. "Indeed."

"So I'll have you fill out an employment application and we'll make plans. When can you start?"

"When do you need me to start?" I asked.

"The sooner the better."

"I could start tomorrow morning."

Wayne looked pleased. "Perfect. Let me show you around."

We both stood and I followed him out of his office. Wayne pointed to a young dark-skinned man at the back of the center near the binding equipment. He was tall, probably six feet three. He looked Indian. "That's Suman," Wayne said. He waved to him and Suman looked up. "Hey, Suman," Wayne shouted, "come here a minute."

The young man checked his machine, then left it running. "What's up, boss?"

"This is Luke. I've just hired him."

I extended my hand. "Pleased to meet you, Su . . ." I struggled with the name.

"Not Sue," he said. "Sooo—mon. It's Bengali. Nice to meet you."

"Suman's my day shift manager," Wayne said. "At least for now. He's got this crazy notion that he's going to run off and be a neurosurgeon."

"I'm out of here in December," he said.

"Where are you going to school?" I asked.

"Johns Hopkins in Maryland."

"Great school," I said.

"Believe it or not," Wayne said to him, "Luke here already knows something about our operation. So put him to work."

"Alrighty," he said. "Come on, I'll give you a tour of the place."

Giving me a tour of a Crisp's copy center would be like guiding the pope through the Vatican. I remembered sitting in my father's conference room playing with an Etch A Sketch when the original copy center layout was designed. Without exception, every center in America followed that plan. I could have drawn the center with my eyes closed.

We walked back to the northeast corner of the store. "Bathrooms are back there near our break room. These are our color digital printers and large format printers, where we do our color copies, oversize prints and banners." The young man who had greeted me when I came in was standing next to one of the machines making a large banner. He looked up at us as we approached.

"That's Colby," Suman said.

I waved. "Hey."

"Hey back," Colby said.

"This is Luke," Suman said. "Wayne just hired him."

"That was fast," Colby said. "No flies on Wayne."

"Wayne, Suman and Colby," I said.

"And there's one more on the day shift. Rachael." Suman started walking again. "Over here is our cutting and binding area. And here are our black and white copiers. We'll start you out with the simpler black and white copiers, then, when I think you're ready, I'll train you on the color copiers. Any questions so far?"

I couldn't resist. "One."

"Shoot."

"I noticed that you're still using the Xerox DocuColor 250. I was just wondering why you haven't upgraded to the 700? The 700 has almost double the copy speed of the 250 with a three-hole punch on the fly," I said. "And it can duplex a seventy-pound stock. These 250's are dinosaurs."

Suman looked surprised, or impressed, I couldn't tell which. "We have a 700 coming in January."

"Good. You're going to love it. The duplexing rocks. It can handle one-hundred-ten-pound cover stock without jamming. And the . . ."

"Okay," Suman said, cutting me off. "You *do* know something about this." He stepped along. "Here are the registers. I assume you know how to operate one as well?"

"Yes."

At the front register was a young, dishwater-blond woman. She was maybe in her mid-to-late twenties, not too thin and naturally pretty. She wore little makeup, not enough to conceal the rings under her eyes. I suppose she looked a little frayed around the edges.

"That's Rachael," Suman said. "Hey, Rachael."

She turned around.

"This is Luke. He's the new guy."

"Hi," I said.

"Pleased to meet you," she replied stiffly, then returned to her work.

"Nice to meet you," I said, turning back to Suman.

He shrugged and we walked to the back of the copy area.

"She's a good gal, hard worker, but as guarded as Fort Knox. I've known her for three years and I still don't know her story." He shook his head. "When do you start?"

"Tomorrow morning."

"Awesome. Welcome to Crisp's."

CHAPTER

Thirty-Three

"Losers keep their eyes on the clock.
Winners keep their eyes on the job."
My father used to always say that to me.

✦ Luke Crisp's Diary ✦

The advertisement I designed for the Golden Age ran that Sunday in the *Las Vegas Sun*. By the time I finished my first day at Crisp's and returned to the care center, Carlos had already had twenty-eight phone calls. He was as giddy as a kid on Christmas morning. He hugged me as I walked in, which was unfortunate because my ribs were still sore.

"You rock, bro," he said, "You did it. You sold the place out."

"Does that mean I'm losing my room?" I asked.

"Yes and no. I talked to the center's owner, Mr. Shantz. He's agreed to put you up in the Desert Spring Apartments a block from here if you'll agree to keep helping us with marketing."

I nodded. "No problem," I said. "But I need to talk to you about my employment. I just took another job."

His expression fell. "You're already leaving us?"

"No. I mean, I hope not. I just need to adjust my schedule a little. I got a job at Crisp's. I work there until four, so I could still get back and help Sylvia with dinner—and any marketing you needed."

He looked somewhat relieved. "That will still work. What time do you start work in the morning?"

"Eight."

"What is that, fourteen, fifteen hours a day?"

"Something like that," I said.

"That's a rough schedule, amigo. You sure you can handle that?"

"I've worked that schedule most of my life."

"When do you find time to live?"

I turned to leave. "Don't worry about me, my friend. I've done enough living for a lifetime."

⋆

From a young age my father taught me the value of hard work. Two full-time jobs wasn't cake, but it wasn't going to break me either. In fact, it was a little refreshing to rediscover the person I used to be. The work also kept my mind off my pain. And I had a lot of pain. I had a lot to mourn. I mourned the loss of my previous life, the opportunities I took so much for granted. I mourned Candace and wondered if I'd ever find love again.

But what I mourned the most was the loss of my father. How could I have hurt him the way I had? I missed him. I missed working and planning together. I missed the way we used to communicate without talking. I worried that he might have more problems with his heart. He could die and I wouldn't know. The knowledge that I had brought him so much pain wracked my soul. It's one thing to be careless with money; it's much worse to be careless with someone's heart—especially a heart that has loved you.

As much as I wanted to, I knew that I could never go back to my father. It wasn't because of pride—I had little enough of that left. I could never go back because after all he had done for me, I had betrayed him. I had betrayed his trust. And I'd deserted him when he needed me the most. I couldn't go back because I didn't deserve his love.

CHAPTER

Thirty-Four

*Everyone carries secret burdens.
Everyone. Some people are just
better at hiding them than others.*

✦ Luke Crisp's Diary ✦

I worked to rebuild my life. I got a new cell phone, a new driver's license and I opened a savings account at a bank a block south of the copy center. I couldn't say I had my life back—what I had had was gone forever—but my life was definitely on the upswing.

It felt good to have some extra money. It felt safe. I was frugal again—as my father was and as I had once been. I ate most of my meals at the Golden Age. I'd even take dinner leftovers from the center to Crisp's to save money on lunch the next day. With no rent, and barely any food expenses, I was able to put away most of my paycheck.

I also got the bonus from Carlos that I'd been promised. My ad had brought in thirteen new residents, so I received a bonus check for $6,500. I bought a car—an old Honda Civic that had belonged to Sylvia's sister. "Looks like junk, runs like a kitten," Sylvia said. It had a thousand scratches and a dent in the passenger-side door, but for just $700 I couldn't go wrong.

As I began reassembling my financial world, I had a thought—I knew there was no way to recover my money from Sean, but I had once read that some gambling losses are tax-deductible. I wondered if I could get a refund on some of the money I'd paid in taxes from my trust. Or, at the least, deduct it from the taxes I would be paying now. I texted Mike Semken and asked him to look into it for me, though I wasn't sure he'd do it since I wasn't really a client of his anymore. I was willing to try anything.

Carlos and Carmen invited me over for Thanksgiving dinner. Their home was a stucco, adobe-style house in the Silverado Ranch area—humble and outdated, full of pictures of their family, avocado green shag carpet and a lot of love. Carlos and Carmen had four children; Duane, Felicia, Barnard and Miguel, in that order. The eldest three were married, providing Carlos and Carmen with five grandchildren.

His oldest son, Duane, looked frail and smaller than his two male siblings, even though he was the oldest and Miguel was still only in high school. Carlos told me that two years earlier Duane had been diagnosed with cardiomyopathy, a condition that would eventually require open heart surgery to prolong his life. Duane owned a landscaping business and had no health insurance when he was diagnosed. As a preexisting condition, no insurance company would cover him and at a cost of more than a quarter million dollars, his chances for treatment seemed unlikely at best. He had applied for Medicaid, but the bureaucratic wheels turned slowly. Duane had a wife, Tasha, and two boys. Carlos was afraid that his son would die before he got treatment.

After dinner I was helping Carmen with the dishes when I asked her about Duane's situation. Her eyes welled up with tears. "We have faith that God will provide," she said, wiping her eyes with a dishcloth. "We hold to that."

CHAPTER

Thirty-Five

One of my associates at Crisp's is named Rachael.
She is quiet, sad and beautiful.
I'm not sure why, but I'd like to get to know her better.

✦ Luke Crisp's Diary ✦

November passed quietly into December. At Crisp's, Suman was preparing to make his departure the week before Christmas. I was going to be sad to see him go. He was a good guy with a wry sense of humor. He ran a solid and profitable day shift but still found time to make it enjoyable, mostly by pranking Colby. I think the most ingenious prank of his was when he froze Mentos candy in ice cubes then dropped them in Colby's Diet Coke when he wasn't looking. It took nearly fifteen minutes before Colby's coke exploded. Colby never figured out what happened.

Wayne spent a lot of time with me going over the shop's clients and finances, things I sometimes had to pretend not to understand, and it became obvious to me that he was priming me to take Suman's position. I learned from Suman that Rachael had seniority, but even though she could undoubtedly use the increased salary that came with the position, she would likely be passed over for the job. She worked hard, but she seemed to lack drive and too many of their customers had complained about her being unfriendly and aloof.

I understood the complaints. Rachael was a mystery to me.

Actually, she was a mystery to everyone at Crisp's, customers and employees alike. She was always quiet and heavy-minded, the way one gets when dealing with heartache. She was cautious like Candace, but that's where the similarities ended. Where Candace was brutally honest, Rachael seemed to conceal everything, cloaking her feelings beneath a thick veil of privacy. Where Candace would dress, or make herself up to accentuate her beauty, Rachael did the opposite. She was beautiful in spite of herself and acted as if she considered her attractiveness more curse than blessing, as she got hit on daily by Crisp's customers. She usually just ignored their advances, but sometimes the veil would part and her temper would show. Suman told me that the store had lost more than one customer that way.

The longer I worked with her, the more she intrigued me. It's been my experience that those with the toughest shells have the softest hearts—and I sensed that she was hiding a naked vulnerability under all that armor.

I honestly had no idea what she thought of me. Our working relationship was cordial, but stiff as a starched collar. One time I caught her looking at me. I knew she had been looking at me for a while, but when I turned to look at her, she quietly turned away. I just couldn't figure her out.

One afternoon I decided to go to the In-N-Out Burger on my break to get a milkshake and passed Rachael as I was leaving. "I'm going to be gone for a few minutes," I said. "I'm going to get a shake."

"All right," she said.

"Want to come? It's slow, Colby can watch the front."

She looked at me for a moment then said, "No thank you."

"We'll only be a few minutes."

"No thank you," she repeated.

Since this was the longest nonwork-related talk I'd had with her since I had started, I decided to venture into unknown territory. "Is it that you don't like shakes or you don't like me? Because if it's the shake, you can order something else."

"I don't associate with coworkers," she said shortly.

"I associate with you all day," I said.

"You know what I mean."

I looked at her for a moment, then said, "Just so I understand, you would get a shake with me if I quit?"

"You wouldn't want to do that on my account," she said. She turned and walked away.

CHAPTER

Thirty-Six

I am lonely. I am lonely. I am lonely. I am lonely. I am lonely.
How appropriate that I write this to no one.

✦ Luke Crisp's Diary ✦

Between my two jobs I developed a routine. I got up at 6 A.M., exercised, ate a piece of toast, then showered and dressed and went into Crisp's. Saturday mornings I slept in until nine or ten, then ran errands or read. Peculiarly, my weekends weren't a whole lot different than when I was homeless—a lot more comfortable, but just as lonely. My father and I used to go golfing every Saturday. I wished I had him to go golfing with now.

One Saturday night I was doing my shopping at the Food King when I saw Rachael standing in the breakfast foods aisle. A boy, maybe six or seven years old, was hanging on the shopping cart next to her. He was whining. "Why can't we have Cap'n Crunch?"

"The cereal in the bag is cheaper," Rachael said. "It's the same thing."

"No it's not. And it has a toy."

"The toys are dumb. It will just end up in the garbage anyway."

"No it won't. I'll play with it."

"I said, no."

I walked up the aisle. "Hi."

I don't know if she was more surprised or embarrassed to see me. She wore a baseball cap and was wearing sweat pants.

"Do you always shop here?" I asked.

"Mostly."

The little boy stared at me intently.

"Who is this handsome young man?" I asked.

"My son," she said, moving in front of the cart as if to shield him from me.

"I'm Luke," I said, extending my hand past her to the boy. "I work with your mother."

He reached out and shook my hand. "I'm Chris."

"Nice to meet you, Chris." I looked up at Rachael. "Have you had dinner yet?"

"We're shopping for dinner right now."

"I can save you the trouble. Why don't we go next door to Italian Village and get some pizza. My treat."

"Yeah!" Chris shouted. "I want pizza. Can we have pizza, Mom?"

"No," Rachael said. "We need to go home."

The boy's face tightened. "Please? He invited us. He said 'his treat.' That means it's free."

"Nothing's free," she said. She shot me a glance of displeasure, then looked back at her son. "I said, no."

"Please, Mom. Please. We never have it anymore."

"Chris, you're seven years old. You're acting like a five-year-old."

I felt bad for the situation I had created, but I was also a little annoyed by how she was handling it. "Come on," I said. "What's it going to hurt?"

"Please, Mom," the boy continued, "please?"

She groaned in surrender. "Okay, okay, okay. We'll get pizza. Just stop nagging." She looked at me with thinly veiled anger. "I need to finish my shopping," she said.

"I'll wait for you up front," I said.

I finished picking up my essentials, then waited at the front of the store for Rachael. She finished her shopping about ten minutes later. Her checkout was lengthy because she used coupons and questioned the prices of several of her purchases, even putting one of them back. Throughout the process her boy kept looking at me. When she was finally done, she pushed her cart over to me. From her expression I thought she'd changed her mind.

"I need to put my groceries in the car," she said.

I followed her to her car, an older-model Jeep Wrangler with a vinyl roof, put her groceries in the back, then the three of us went to the pizzeria. Chris looked as happy as a boy walking into Disneyland.

The restaurant was crowded, and after a fifteen-minute wait the hostess sat us at a booth in the corner of the restaurant. Rachael was her usual sullen self, which was countered by her son's excited chatter.

"What do you want to eat?" I asked.

"Pizza," Chris said. "With pepperoni."

I looked at Rachael. "And you?"

"I'll just have some of what Chris has."

"Pepperoni pizza it is." I turned to her son. "What grade are you in, Chris?"

"Second grade. I have Covey for my teacher. She's a tool."

"Chris!" Rachael said. "That's not okay."

"She's really mean," he continued. "Once my friend Brian accidentally peed his pants in class, and she made him sit in it until recess."

I looked at Rachael, who was shaking her head.

"I agree with Chris," I said. "Covey is a tool."

"Yeah," Chris said, "she stinks."

"Chris," Rachael said. "Enough of that."

I hid my smile. The waitress brought us a pitcher of root beer, a large pepperoni pizza and an order of cheese-garlic bread. A few minutes after we'd started eating, I asked Rachael, "Have you lived in Las Vegas your whole life?"

"We moved here about eight years ago."

"Where did you live before that?"

"St. George, Utah."

"What brought you to Vegas?"

"My husband," she said. She turned to her son. "Don't take such big bites."

He looked at me and smiled.

Rachael said little for the rest of our dinner, and she was ready to leave before Chris or I were done eating. "We've got to go," she said. "We've got milk in the car."

"Let me get a box for the pizza."

"No, we don't need . . ."

"There's no sense letting it go to waste," I said. "Chris can have it for breakfast."

"You eat pizza for breakfast?" Chris asked.

"Breakfast pizza is the best," I said.

"Cool."

I paid the bill at the counter, then brought back a carry-out box, put the leftover pizza in it and handed it to Chris. "Thanks, Mr. Luke."

"You're welcome, Chris," I said. "I'll see you later."

Rachael said to him, "Honey, wait over there by the door for a minute. I need to talk to Mr. Luke."

"Okay, Mom."

As soon as he was away from us Rachael spun around. Her anger had returned. "Don't you ever do that again. Do you understand me?"

I folded my arms. "Do what?"

"Use my kid to get to me."

"Is that what you think this was about?"

"Of course that's what *this* is about."

I shook my head. "Maybe I just thought it would be nice to get to know someone I have to spend my day with. Maybe I thought we could be friends. Obviously I was mistaken." I looked into her eyes. "There are wild boars with better dispositions."

She looked shocked. When she could speak, she said, "Just stay away from me." She turned and walked away.

"We work together," I said after her. "Good luck with that."

She took the pizza from Chris and walked out to her car. She never looked back.

CHAPTER

Thirty-Seven

As if she didn't already hate me enough,
I was just given Rachael's promotion.
I don't think she'll be sending a congratulatory bouquet.

✦ Luke Crisp's Diary ✦

That next Monday at Crisp's was uncomfortable. Rachael was even more dismal than usual, which is really saying something. The tension was palpable. Just before lunch Wayne called me into his office. I assumed he wanted to ask me what was going on between Rachael and me. As I walked in, Suman was sitting in a chair next to Wayne's desk.

"What's up, guys?" I asked.

Wayne smiled. "Congratulations. You're our new day shift manager."

Suman put out his hand. "Congratulations, man. You'll do a great job."

Oddly, my first thought was less about me getting the job than about Rachael not getting it. For a moment I looked back and forth between them. "Thanks. I wasn't expecting this."

"Of course you were," Wayne said, grinning. "You'll take over the day Suman leaves. Which is . . ."

Suman shook his head. "I've told him like twenty times." He turned back to Wayne. "The twenty-second."

Wayne nodded. "The twenty-second. So Suman will teach you everything you need to know until then."

"He already knows everything," Suman said. "Don't you?" When I didn't respond, he shoved me. "Don't you?"

"Right," I said. I wasn't paying attention. I was thinking about how Rachael would handle the news. "When are you going to tell the others?" I asked.

"I already have," Wayne said. "Colby just found out this morning, but I called Rachael over the weekend and told her. I wanted to give her some time to deal with it."

I wondered if that was before or after our dinner. I could only imagine what Rachael was thinking of me now. "How did she take it?" I asked.

"Honestly, she wasn't real happy. But not surprised either. She'll get over it." He slapped me on the back. "So let's get some lunch to celebrate. My treat. You like sushi?"

"Love sushi," I said.

The three of us stood and walked out of Wayne's office. As we were leaving, Suman said to Rachael, "We're leaving for lunch. You have the floor, Rachael."

"Okay," she said softly. She glanced at me then turned away.

*

Rachael didn't say a word to me the rest of the day. Finally, about an hour before quitting time, I saw her go into the back room for paper. I followed her, shutting the door partially behind me. "Rachael."

"What?" she said without looking at me.

"Look, I'm sorry about what I said to you the other night—

the wild boar thing. That was mean. Can we please just forget about it and move on?"

She turned around. "That's easy for you to say," she said. "Chris talked nonstop about you all day yesterday. He didn't need that *complication* in his life."

"Complication?"

"Yes, complication."

"If he was talking about me all day, maybe that's exactly what he does need."

"You have no idea what my son needs."

"You're right. I have no idea. It's just unfortunate that he had such a good time that he wanted to talk about it all day. What an awful thing."

Her eyes narrowed. "Do you think this is a joke?"

"No. I think the way you're handling this is a joke. Do you think you're the only one with problems? You think you're the only one who has ever been *betrayed*?"

She bristled at the word. "I didn't say anything about being betrayed."

"You don't need to. Why else would you wear that much armor?"

She stood there staring at me, speechless. "I have nothing to say to you. Now please let me by."

I stepped sideways. "By all means."

"Oh, and congratulations on your promotion." She pushed past me and went back out to the front counter.

I followed her out. "Is that what this is about?"

"No. I didn't care for you before you stole my job."

"Stole? It was yours to lose."

"What is that supposed to mean?"

"It means you didn't deserve it. You know what? You make people feel bad. Whatever the world did to you, you're certainly giving it back."

"I could never give back that much." Her eyes welled up with tears, and for the first time I saw just how deeply she had been hurt. I regretted my comment. She looked down, covering her eyes with her hand. "Please, just leave me alone."

I looked at her, wanting to say something, wanting to apologize, but I knew she didn't want me to. I walked away from her. She didn't look at me again the rest of our shift, and she disappeared quickly at quitting time.

CHAPTER

Thirty-Eight

Sometimes it's not strength but gentleness
that cracks the hardest shells.

✦ Luke Crisp's Diary ✦

My job at the Golden Age changed as well. We had lost several residents in November and I helped Carlos quickly fill the vacancies. The facility had, for the first time ever, a waiting list to get in. I think Carlos sensed that I wasn't going to be able to keep up both jobs forever, so rather than lose me, he changed the deal. The day after my promotion at Crisp's he brought me into his office.

"What's up?"

"How do you feel about feeding residents?"

I shrugged. "It's not really my career path, but with the kind of money you're paying me, it's hard to give up."

He smiled. "Well, I have a better offer. I'll pay you the same monthly salary as you make now if you'll come on as my marketing director for two afternoons a week—you pick the days. I just need you to keep helping Sylvia until the twenty-third. That's when I've got some new people starting."

"I still get meals?"

"Meals, apartment, laundry, everything. Heck, you can still wear scrubs if you want."

"You drive a hard bargain, my friend. But you've got yourself a deal."

✳

The twenty-second of December was Suman's last day at Crisp's. Around lunchtime we had a small going-away party to celebrate his new adventure. Wayne had purchased ice cream and a devil's food cake at the grocery store down the street. He hadn't checked the cake at the store so he didn't notice until he opened the cake box at Crisp's that they had misspelled Suman's name. The cake read:

Bon Voyage, Shoe Man

Wayne was pretty upset by the mistake and overly apologetic. Suman thought it was hilarious. He took a picture of the cake with his phone and insisted on having the piece with his misspelled name. He took the cake, climbed up on a chair and sang in his best John Lennon, "I am the shoe man, I am the shoe man, I am the loafer, goo, goo, g'joob."

Rachael didn't attend the party. Rather than trading off, as we usually did for internal events, Rachael volunteered to stay out front the whole time. I didn't like that she had excluded herself and I kept looking out at her. I took her a piece of cake that she refused with a simple, "I'm on a diet."

Wayne noticed my concern and pulled me aside. "Look, Luke. You're the right person for this job. Rachael had every opportunity for the promotion and she blew it. In fact, I put her on probation. I told her if she doesn't change her attitude we may have to let her go."

This didn't make me feel any better. We were winding up our party when we heard an angry customer shouting up front. Suman turned to me. "You're up to bat, manager."

"Thanks, shoe man," I said, shoving a final bite of cake into my mouth, then throwing my plate into the trash. I walked out front to see what was going on. A heavyset man in a dark business suit was standing at the front counter yelling at Rachael. The man was red-faced and looked like he was about to burst a blood vessel in his neck.

I walked up to the counter. "Excuse, me, sir. May I help you?"

"I doubt anyone around here is competent enough to help anyone," he said. He waved a finger in Rachael's face. "This is the last time I bring my business here. Do you understand? Last time."

"Sir," I said calmly, "please tell me what's wrong."

He turned to face me, waving a piece of paper in the air. "I brought this job in yesterday to have printed. I specifically asked this woman for one-sided copies. Instead, I have printing on both sides. I can't use this. My conference begins in one hour at the Tropicana."

"Let me see," I said. I examined the fliers, then looked over the order form. The job was marked for double-sided printing. Rachael had incorrectly marked the order form.

I looked back up. "I can see why you're upset. You're absolutely right, this was supposed to be printed single-sided. But it's not her fault, sir. It was mine. I'm new here and I got the order wrong. But more important than my incompentency, is that you need your handouts right away. I'll pull the job I have on the copier right now and get your order for you in fifteen minutes. Will that give you enough time to get back to the Tropicana? Or do you need to get back and have me hand deliver them to you?"

He calmed down a little. "I suppose I can wait fifteen minutes. Just hurry."

"Of course. Fifteen minutes. Tell you what," I said. I pulled out my wallet. "You don't want to stand around here waiting, there's an In-N-Out Burger across the parking lot. They have the best strawberry shake you'll ever try. I practically live on them." I offered him three dollars. "Go get yourself a shake on me. By the time you're back, I'll have your job done, boxed and ready to run. Since it's already been billed to your account, I'll credit back a fifty percent discount for your inconvenience. You just need to sign the pickup form. Now go get one of those shakes."

He looked at my dollars waving in front of him. "You don't need to . . ."

"Please. I'm embarrassed. It would really be doing me a favor."

He awkwardly took the cash. "All right. I am a little hungry. I'll be back in fifteen minutes." Then he added, "Thank you."

"Please," I said. I took the order back and put it on the machine. A couple minutes after he was gone, Rachael walked back. "That wasn't your mistake."

"I know."

She stood there for a moment, then turned and walked back to the front. The man was back in less than fifteen minutes. I had already printed the handouts, boxed them and given them to Rachael. She handed them over the counter. "Here you go, sir."

The man was calm as he took the box. "I apologize again for my mistake," I said. "I hope I didn't cause too much of an inconvenience."

"No, I've still got time. Everything will be fine. Thank you."

"My pleasure. See you next time."

"You bet you will." He started to turn then stopped. "What's your name?"

"It's Luke."

"Luke, if you ever need a job in customer service, I'm hiring."

"You flatter me, sir."

"You're good," he said, shaking his head. "By the way, that shake really was good."

"Nectar of the gods," I said.

The man laughed as he walked out. After he was gone, Wayne walked up to me. "What was that about?"

"Nothing. We mixed up a job of his. But it's handled."

His brow rose. "*We?*"

I looked into his eyes. "*I got it wrong.*"

He looked at me suspiciously. "Really? That's a first."

"Everyone makes mistakes. Even me."

"Do you know who that was?"

"A customer."

"He's Charles Cunningham with Omega—one of our most important accounts."

"I thought they were all important."

He grinned. "You are good."

✦

The rest of the afternoon went without incident. Rachael left work before me and without a word. As I was walking out to my car, Rachael shouted to me. "Luke."

I turned around. She was standing up against the building.

"What's up?" I asked.

She walked up to me, brushing a strand of hair from her face. "Why did you do that? Why did you take the blame?"

"It's good business. I'm the new guy. Everyone expects the new guy to screw up."

"But you didn't."

I just looked at her for a moment and then said, "You look like you could use a break. Everyone needs a break now and then. It's no big deal." I turned to go.

"Luke. I'm sorry."

I turned back. "Me too."

"Can we get a coffee?"

"You don't owe me."

"That's not why." She looked down for a moment. When she looked back up, her eyes were wet with tears. "I could use a friend too."

For the first time since I'd met her, she looked vulnerable. "I can't do anything now, I have my other job. But I can when I get off work later tonight."

"When's that?"

"Around ten."

"Okay," she said, slightly nodding. "I'll give you my number."

"I have it," I said.

She looked surprised. "You do?"

"I'm the manager."

"Of course. I'll see you later. Thank you." She turned and walked slowly to her car.

CHAPTER

Thirty-Nine

To open the book of another's life requires great care,
as the pages must be turned with delicacy and caution—
but it is usually worth the effort.

✦ Luke Crisp's Diary ✦

I finished work then called Rachael and we arranged to meet at a coffee shop near her home. She was already there when I arrived. I paid for two large coffees and carried them to a vacant corner near the back of the shop. We sat down at a round-topped table for two. Rachael seemed a little anxious, so I started the conversation with a couple softballs. "Who's watching Chris tonight?"

"I have a neighbor in our apartment building who watches him while I work. She has a son his age, so it works out."

"How long have you worked at Crisp's?" I asked.

"About three years. I started right after . . ." she stopped. "About three years."

"That's a while."

"Well, they've been good to me. Chris has some health problems and I can't get insurance anywhere else that will cover them. But Crisp's has full coverage."

"Do you mind me asking what kind of health problems?"

She hesitated. "Emotional ones. He sees a counselor every week. And he takes some medications for ADHD."

I nodded sympathetically. "He's a likable kid."

"He's a good kid," she said. "No child should have to

go through what he's gone through." She looked at me. "The man who owns Crisp's is a family man. He takes care of us."

"He's a good man," I said.

"You say that like you know him."

I paused. "I've met him," I said.

"I'd like to meet him someday," she said. "I'd like to thank him." She stirred her coffee. "I have a question for you. Why do you know so much about the copy center?"

"I'll tell you, but . . ."

"You'll have to kill me?"

I laughed. "No. But you have to promise to never tell anyone."

"I can do that."

"I used to be a regional manager for Crisp's. I managed twelve stores."

She looked at me in surprise. "Does Wayne know that?"

"No."

"Why wouldn't you tell him?"

I thought about how to answer. "I have my reasons."

She looked vexed. "Did something happen?"

"You could say that." I took a drink of my coffee.

"You're not going to tell me," she said.

"I'd rather not."

"Fair enough," she said, lifting her cup.

"So let's talk about you," I said.

"What do you want to know?"

"Where's Chris's father?"

Her expression fell. She set her cup down.

"I'm sorry," I said. "That was abrupt. You don't have to tell me."

She looked down for a long time and I couldn't tell what she was thinking. Then she said, "He took his life." Her eyes began to well up. I reached over and took her hand. When she could speak, she said, "My husband, Rex, sold real estate. We came to Vegas because the real estate market was exploding down here. At first it was great. We were making more money than I ever dreamed we'd make. We bought a nice little place in Henderson. Rex bought himself a custom Corvette. Things were going really well." She wiped her eyes with a napkin.

"We were going to wait to have a baby until we were better established, but with all the money, I didn't need to work, so I got pregnant.

"A couple years after Chris was born, Rex started working late all the time. Then he started bringing less money home. Not too much, but enough that we had to cut back. He told me that the market had gotten tighter and he had to work more to try to keep up with our expenses.

"What he didn't tell me is that he had developed a gambling addiction. He had started gambling with some of his clients and it just got out of control. He started spending all his lunch breaks at casinos. It went on for years.

"He started acting different. I had no idea what was going on. At first I thought that maybe he was having an affair. If someone had told me what he was really doing, I wouldn't have believed them. When we were dating, the only card games he knew were Go Fish and Solitaire. I don't think that he had ever even tried a slot machine.

"But once he was hooked, everything changed. He started missing his appointments and he got fired from the agency he worked for. Then, as things got worse, some of our things started disappearing around the house. One day I came home and someone had broken in. Our TVs, computers and jewelry were all gone. I should have suspected something, since whoever broke in seemed to know where everything was.

"Then, a month later, my wedding ring disappeared. I thought it was our house cleaners, but I couldn't prove it. I fired them. We couldn't afford them anymore anyway, but even after they were gone, things kept disappearing.

"Then one day I opened a credit card statement. My first thought was, there's some mistake here. We don't have a Discover card. It was maxed out to twenty-five thousand dollars and the monthly payment was late. I called the company. But they wouldn't talk to me because I wasn't on the account. I was waiting for Rex when he got home. That's when he confessed to the gambling. I pressed him on how much he owed. He lied at first. He said it was only the twenty-five thousand on the card. But I went online and pulled up our IRA and retirement accounts. He had drained them all. I freaked out and started hitting him. Then I kicked him out of the house."

"I understand," I said. "I knew someone who had a gambling problem. It almost cost him his life."

"It's a pernicious evil," she said, slowly shaking her head.

"Is that when he took his life?"

"No. He called me every day for the next month, begging for a second chance. Chris missed him. The truth is, I missed him. I finally told him that if he'd promise to never gamble again and get professional help, I'd take him back. He agreed. He started attending a Gamblers Anonymous group in the area.

"Things started to get back on track. Rex started to bring home more money and we started saving a little again. After six months he was even leading one of the GA groups in the area.

"We had our life back. At least for a while. Then one day I got a visit from the Vegas police. Rex had jumped from the seventh floor of a casino parking garage."

"I'm sorry."

She let out a long sigh. "After I identified the body, I came back and started checking our accounts. In all, Rex had maxed out fourteen credit cards, taken a second mortgage on our home and maxed out his expense account at work. I figured he'd lost more than four hundred thousand dollars. A few weeks later I found out that he hadn't paid our taxes in two years.

"The IRS came after me of course. I was bankrupt. Chris and I lost our home and our car. I sold what I could, found an apartment and got a job." She looked at me with pained eyes. "You think these things only happen to people on television, but they happen to real people. And they happen all the time. You just don't hear about it. My husband was the fourth person to jump from that parking garage that month."

"How old was Chris when this happened?"

"He was four."

"No wonder he's having problems."

"Yeah, it's no surprise." After a moment she said, "You know, I didn't really hate you. I wanted to get to know you better. But the frightened half of me just kept shutting me down. I just didn't want to trust again."

"I can understand why you wouldn't trust."

"Trust," she said again, like the word was sour on her tongue. She stirred her drink. "You know what I hated most of all about it? Even more than all the money he lost? Maybe even more than his suicide? It was his dishonesty. He hid everything from me. And I was stupid enough to trust him."

"Trust isn't stupid."

"Sometimes it is." She took a slow sip from her coffee, set down her cup and wiped her eyes. "So a very long answer to a short question."

"Thank you for telling me."

"I've never told anyone at work," she said. "I just don't think they need to know."

"They don't," I said.

She took another sip of her drink, then asked, "Have you ever been married?"

"No. Almost." I looked into her eyes. "There's something you don't know about me. I used to have a lot of money. But I lost it all."

"How did you lose it?"

"You name it. Taxes, the stock market," I said. "Mostly bad

judgment. I was here, in Vegas, with the girl I thought I was going to marry, when I found out I was bankrupt. When she found out I was broke, she left."

"I'm sorry," Rachael said.

"Me too," I said. "In retrospect, I suppose it's for the better. I never would have known who she really was if I hadn't lost everything."

"It still hurts to lose someone," Rachael said. "I still miss Rex. I wish we had just remained poor. We were happy then. Our happiest time was when we were struggling together, trying to make ends meet."

"Wow," I said. "That's exactly why Candace left me."

"Her name is Candace?"

I nodded.

"That's a pretty name."

"She's a pretty girl. But she didn't want to go through those times. She said it would ruin us."

"Not if you love each other," Rachael said.

"That's a good answer," I replied. I looked at her thoughtfully for a few moments then asked, "Are you lonely?"

She smiled sadly, then replied, "Chris keeps me so busy, and with work . . ."

"You didn't answer my question," I said.

She smiled a little. "In the worst way."

"Me too. So, what are you doing for Christmas?"

CHAPTER

Forty

I dreamt last night that I had gone home to my father's house for Christmas. But even though the lights were on, the doors were locked. I rang the doorbell and knocked, but no one answered. I looked through the front window. The house was crowded with people and presents. There was music and laughter. In the center of it all, I could see my father. He turned and looked at me, then turned away. No matter how many times I knocked, he wouldn't open the door. He wouldn't let me in.

✦ Luke Crisp's Diary ✦

Rachael and I decided to spend Christmas together. As we talked that night, I learned that she hadn't bought much for Chris for Christmas. She couldn't afford to.

"I think we should go out Christmas shopping," I said.

"I really can't afford to buy anything more."

"I know, but I can. I got this big bonus at my other job."

"That's sweet of you," Rachael said, "but you really don't need to do that."

"I have no one to give anything to. What kind of Christmas is that? You'll be doing me a favor."

A smile crossed her lips. "Okay. But only a few things."

I picked Rachael up early the morning of Christmas Eve and we went to the mall. Shopping on Christmas Eve is never safe, but when it falls on a Saturday, it's practically hand-to-hand combat. In spite of the insanity, we managed to get everything Chris had asked for and then some. Afterward we stopped for lunch.

"The malls were crazy," Rachael said. "People are so dumb to leave their shopping to the last minute."

"By 'people,'" I said, "you're including us, right?"

She laughed. "I guess so."

"So, dummy, what do you want to do tonight?"

"I was planning on baking Christmas cookies and taking them to neighbors."

"Sounds fun. What about Christmas dinner tomorrow? What should we make?"

"We?" Rachael asked. "Can you cook?"

"I'm a terrific cook," I said. "I make a mean three-cheese lasagna. I don't even need the recipe. I've got it up here." I pointed to my head.

"I love lasagna," Rachael said. "So does Christopher."

"I've got an idea. How about we have an Italian Christmas dinner? Lasagna, bruschetta, cantaloupe with prosciutto. I'll cook."

She looked at me in amazement. "Really? You'll make Christmas dinner?"

"The whole thing. You don't even have to help."

"May I help if I want to?"

"If you're dying to."

"I might be," she said. "It sounds fun."

"Great. Italian it is. This will be a Christmas to remember."

After lunch we drove to the supermarket, which was nearly as crowded as the mall. It was the same market where I'd invited Rachael and Chris to pizza and incurred Rachael's wrath. We bought premade butter-cream frosting and sprinkles for the cookies, lasagna noodles, hamburger and ricotta, cheddar and parmesan cheese, a bottle of wine, a loaf of Italian bread, garlic, cantaloupe and prosciutto crudo, sun-dried tomatoes, goat cheese and crostini.

"What is this?" Rachael asked, looking at the prosciutto.

"Prosciutto crudo. It's Italian ham."

"It doesn't look like ham."

"That's because it's raw. It's *crudo*."

"How do you cook it?"

I smiled. "You don't. You eat it like that."

"Raw?"

"Think of it as pig sushi."

She stared at me as if trying to determine if I was teasing her or not. "You're making this up."

"No, I'm not. It's good. Sixty million Italians can't be wrong. Unless you're talking about politics. Or plumbing. Anyway, it's really good with cantaloupe. Trust me. You'll like it."

"Okay," she said. "I'll trust you."

We drove back to Rachael's apartment, put away the groceries and hid the presents we'd bought in the hall closet, then picked up Chris from the neighbors a couple doors down the hallway. Chris ran and jumped on me when he saw me.

"He's starved for male attention," Rachael said, and then added, "I guess that makes two of us."

Chris and I played on his Playstation while Rachael made the cookie dough. She rolled out the dough on her counter, then we cut out the cookies with cookie cutters shaped like candy canes and holly leaves and laid them out on baking sheets. After they were baked, we let them cool, then frosted them with the white butter-cream frosting, and Chris decorated the cookies with red and green sprinkles. We put most of the cookies on plates (after eating at least a dozen of them ourselves) and delivered them to Rachael's neighbors in the apartment complex. Then we drove over to Carlos and Carmen's house.

Carlos answered the door. I introduced him to Rachael and Chris, then he invited us inside. Carmen was in the kitchen cooking. Two of their grandchildren were at her feet. "Look, kids," Carlos said, "Mr. Crisp brought some Christmas cookies."

The children jumped up in excitement, screaming in unison, "I want one! I want one!"

Chris held out the plate for them.

"Just one for now," Carmen warned.

"Are these Duane's kids?" I asked.

Carlos nodded. "Yes, he's not feeling well tonight. Tasha's at home taking care of him." I saw sadness come into his eyes. I didn't ask anything more about Duane.

CHAPTER

Forty-One

Oftentimes, the greatest peace comes of surrender.

✦ Luke Crisp's Diary ✦

Carlos and Carmen asked us to stay and visit, and it was after eleven when we finally got back to Rachael's. Chris fell asleep on the ride back and I carried him up to the apartment. Rachael had me put him in her bed. "He needs his pills," she said. She left the room, returning with two pills and a cup of water.

"He takes them at night?"

"Two at night," she said. "Three in the morning." She lifted him up. "Come on, son," she said. "Take your pills." He woke enough to swallow the tablets, then she helped him into his pajamas, kissed him and tucked him in bed. He immediately fell back asleep.

Rachael shut the bedroom door, and we took the presents out of the hall closet and wrapped them in the front room. Then we laid them under the Christmas tree—a small Douglas fir strung with silver garlands and small, blinking, multicolored lights. The presents filled the entire corner of the room. We sat on the couch and looked at the tree.

"You said you were only going to buy a few things," she said.

"I lied."

"You certainly did," she said. "You're on Santa's bad list."

"That's certain," I said. I looked at the tree and sighed. "There are few things as peaceful as a Christmas tree." I leaned back into the sofa. "The Christmas before my mother died, I asked her if I could sleep on the couch in front of the tree."

"What did she say?"

"She said yes." Rachael smiled. I looked at her. "It's nice to see you smile."

Her smile grew a little more. "It's nice to want to smile." She looked into my eyes. "This has been a good day."

"Me too."

"That doesn't make any sense," she said.

"I know," I said. "I'm tired."

She sighed happily and looked at the tree. "Look at all those presents. He's going to be so excited." Her smile softened. "It's been a long time since he's had a good Christmas." She turned to me. "The Christmas after Rex died, I asked Chris what he wanted for Christmas. He told me that Santa was bringing his daddy back. I told him that that wasn't possible. But he had seen some movie at school where a little girl had asked Santa for her daddy back and he miraculously came back. He said to me, 'You just have to believe, Mommy.'"

"Oh no," I said.

"He was only five years old. It broke my heart."

"He's lucky to have you," I said.

"I'm all he has." After a few minutes she asked, "Do you have any brothers or sisters?"

"No. I'm an only child."

"Me too," Rachael said. "Is your father still alive?"

"Yes."

"Why aren't you spending Christmas with him?"

"He . . ." I wasn't sure what to say. "He's not talking to me anymore."

"I'm sorry," she said.

"Me too. He was my best friend."

✦

We sat a little while longer in silence, the tree lights illuminating the room. I'm not sure of the hour, it was late and I was exhausted, but it felt so good to be with her I didn't want to leave even though I kept dozing off. At one point I woke myself snoring. Rachael laughed. "You're tired."

"Two jobs is killing me," I said. "I better get home while I can still drive."

Rachael frowned. "Okay," she said. She stood and took my hand to pull me up from the couch. Instead, I pulled her back and she fell on top of me, laughing. Then she stopped, our faces inches apart, our eyes locked on each other. "Will you kiss me?" she asked quietly.

I pulled her into me and we softly kissed. Her lips were warm and moist and tasted of candy cane lip gloss. After a minute she pulled away, her eyes still closed, as if she was still savoring what we'd just shared. When she opened her eyes, she said nothing, but stood, looking at me with a kind of sweet reverence. She took my hand again, and this time I stood and we walked to the door still holding hands.

At the door she leaned into me and we kissed again, this time much longer. When we finally separated, Rachael put her cheek against my shoulder and I pulled her into me. Her body felt so warm and soft against mine. After a few minutes she stepped back from me and looked into my eyes. In spite of the hour, her eyes were bright. "Merry Christmas, Luke."

"Merry Christmas," I said.

"What time are you coming over tomorrow?"

"Whenever you want. Do you want me to come over early?"

She nodded happily. "It would be fun to have you here when Chris opens his presents."

"What time will Chris be up?"

She grinned. "Three," she said. "But I make him wait until the sun's up."

"Okay," I said. "I'll be over by sunrise."

She put her head back against my shoulder. "May I ask you something?" she said.

"Sure."

"Am I really as mean as a wild boar?"

I laughed. "No. You're more like a piglet."

She playfully hit me. "Thanks." She leaned back and quickly kissed me again, then stepped back. "Good night."

"Good night, Rachael. Have pleasant dreams."

A warm smile blanketed her face. "I will."

I stepped out into the hallway, looked back at her once more. She smiled and waved and shut the door. I walked out to my car with a big smile on my face.

CHAPTER

Forty-Two

I feel as excited as a child on Christmas morning—
and probably for many of the same reasons.

✦ Luke Crisp's Diary ✦

Morning came early. I was probably just as excited to wake as Chris was. I was excited to see Rachael again. In the haze of my waking I began to believe that I had dreamt the last moments of our night together, until I fully woke. No, we had actually kissed. I could still taste her lip gloss on my lips. I quickly showered and dressed and drove over to Rachael's apartment as the first streaks of dawn lit the morning sky.

Rachael answered the door in her robe. While I was still in the hallway, she looked over her shoulder to make sure that Chris hadn't come into the front room, then we kissed again.

"Do you know how good that feels?" she asked.

"Yes," I said.

She took my hand and led me to her bedroom, dropping my hand at the door. Chris was awake, sitting upright on the bed.

"Hi, Luke!" Chris said.

"Hi, buddy," I said. "Ready to see if Santa came?"

"Not so fast," Rachael said. "We have a tradition. We read from the Bible before we go out and see what Santa has brought."

"Your name is Luke," Chris said. "Just like in the Bible."

"Just like it," I said.

We took turns reading from the second chapter of Luke from verses 1 to 14. The millisecond I finished reading the last verse, "Glory to God in the highest, and on earth peace, good will toward men," Chris shouted, "Let's go!"

Rachael said, "Wait, let me get my camera."

"Hurry, Mom," Chris said. "It's torture."

Rachael went into the front room and stood there, ready to snap Chris's picture as he walked in. "All right," she said. "Come on."

Chris ran down the short hall. He stopped at the edge of the front room, staring at all the presents. "No way," he said.

Rachael and I sat on the couch watching Chris open his presents. Each opening elicited an excited response, followed by "Mom! Luke! Look at this!"

When he'd finished opening all his presents, he collected them all in a big pile, then sat down and began playing with a box of LEGOs.

"I'm going to make breakfast," Rachael said. "Do you like blueberry muffins?"

I nodded.

"Luke, come help me build," Chris said.

"Chris," Rachael said. "Luke's probably tired."

"That's okay," I said. "There's work to be done."

✦

I helped Chris build a LEGO monster insect (or something like that) until Rachael called us for breakfast. After eating I helped Chris take his presents into his room. When I came back out, Rachael was gathering up wrapping paper into a garbage sack.

"You look tired," she said.

"I'm exhausted. You've been working me like a rented mule."

She laughed. "If you lie down," she said. "I'll rub your back."

"You talked me into it." I lay down on the couch. Rachael sat on the floor next to me.

At first Rachael massaged my shoulders and back, then she put her hand under my shirt and began running her long nails gently up and down my back, then up my neck and to my head. "Is that okay?" she whispered.

"Never, ever stop," I said.

I don't know how long I lay there before I fell asleep. When I woke, Rachael was asleep on the floor next to the couch. I woke her as I sat up. She looked around. "Oh, I fell asleep," she said. "Where's Christopher?"

"Probably still in his room," I said. I checked my watch. It was almost one. "I better get started on dinner."

"I'll help," she said.

It took us about two hours to prepare everything while Chris played contentedly in his room. We still had a few hours to kill, so I suggested we go for a drive.

A week earlier I had asked Sylvia about things to do in Las Vegas over the holidays, and she went to the city Web site and printed me out an entire list. The first stop on her list was the Bellagio Hotel. At Christmastime, the fountains in front of the hotel are choreographed to Christmas music.

The strip was bustling with humanity. All the casinos remain open on Christmas Day, and there was a sizable crowd accumulated outside the Bellagio to watch the fountains. As I looked at the hotel, I felt a sense of dread. *Why had I come back here?*

As I was pulling into the hotel's parking lot, I said to Rachael, "This is where I was staying when I found out I was broke." I pointed to the grove of trees. "That's where I got robbed."

All she said was, "I hate the casinos."

There was real pain in her voice. Stupidly, I hadn't even thought about how much spending Christmas Day on the strip would bother her.

"Of course," I said. "I'm sorry. We'll go."

We left the strip and, in a moment of weakness, drove to the corner of Pecos and Sunset to Wayne Newton's home, which was decked out for the holidays. Then we headed back to the apartment for dinner.

I put the lasagna in to bake while Rachael cut the cantaloupe into wedges, which I then draped with thin slices of prosciutto.

I thought about my father. He, Mary, Barbara and Paul would be done eating by now. He'd probably be in the den talking to Paul. I wondered if he would talk about me. I felt incredibly homesick. I was grateful that I wasn't alone.

Our Italian Christmas meal turned out perfect. Rachael and Chris both had seconds and Chris had thirds on the lasagna. After eating we watched a Christmas show on television—the one with Ralphie and his Red Ryder BB gun—then Rachael gave Chris his pills and sent him to bed. He hugged me before leaving the room. "Can you come back tomorrow?" he said.

I looked at Rachael. "We'll see," I said.

"We have to go back to work tomorrow, honey," she said. Chris frowned and she added, "But we'll see."

After Chris was asleep, Rachael and I went back to the living room. We turned off the overhead lights so the room was only lit by the flashing lights of the tree. Everything was quiet. Peaceful. I stretched out on the sofa with my arms around Rachael, who was lying in front of me. After five or so minutes of silence, Rachael turned around and said, "Thank you."

Instead of asking what she was thanking me for, I pulled her into me, kissing her forehead.

"You have bad aim," she said, touching my lips with her finger. "My lips are down here."

I kissed her on the lips. We kissed for a few minutes.

After we parted, she said, "Are you always like this?"

"Like what?"

"Sweet."

"Not always," I said.

She was quiet for a moment, and then she said, "You know you're my manager now. This is total sexual harassment."

"You're right," I said. "We better stop." I started to pull away from her and she clung to me.

"Where do you think you're going?"

"I have no idea," I said.

"Neither do I," she said. Then her voice dropped. She asked, "Are we going somewhere with this?"

The question caught me off guard. After a moment I said, "I don't know."

She kissed my cheek. "Even if we're not, I wouldn't change a thing. These have been my best days in years." Her eyes began welling up and a tear rolled down her cheek. I touched her cheek, tracing the wet where the tear had fallen.

"What's wrong?" I asked.

"I was afraid I might fall for you." As she looked into my eyes, I saw the vulnerable little girl inside of her. "I just ask one thing. Please be honest with me. And if you don't want me, just tell me. Okay?"

"You don't need to be afraid," I said.

"It's not just me. I think Chris has fallen for you too. It's one thing to take chances with your own heart. It's another thing to take chances with your son's."

"You're a good mother," I said.

"I wonder sometimes."

"All good parents wonder. That's what makes them good."

We were both quiet again. A few minutes later Rachael asked, "Do you remember what your mother was like?"

I nodded. "She was good," I said. "I'm sure my memory is skewed, but I find myself thinking of her as a fifties TV sitcom mother. She was always cheerful. She'd be there with a plate of cookies, waiting for me to come home from school."

"What's your father like?"

"He's good too. He has a good heart. Some people compartmentalize their lives between home and business. My father wasn't that way. He was the same man at the office as he was at home. I think he cared as much about the people he worked with as he did about himself."

"You admired him?"

"I still admire him."

"Then why aren't you speaking to each other?"

"It's all my fault. I hurt him. I ignored his wishes, squandered his money and left him when he needed me the most." I looked into her eyes. "He said I was dead to him."

After a moment she said, "Then we have something in common. We're both dead to our parents. My parents disowned me when I married Rex."

"Why didn't they like Rex?"

"He didn't belong to our church," she said.

I thought about this. "Now that he's gone, is there any chance of reconciliation?"

"I don't know if I want to," she said sadly. "I think it's probably too late anyway. They missed my wedding, Chris's birth and Rex's funeral, which I'm sure, in their minds, was God's retribution for my choices.

"For the longest time I hated them. But now I just pity them. In their hearts they've consigned most of God's children to Hell and believe they're righteous for doing so." She looked into my eyes. "They've never even seen their only grandchild. Can you believe that?"

I shook my head.

"I just don't understand that mentality. If I thought Chris was headed to Hell, the last thing I'd do is abandon him. The truth is, I think a place filled with people like them *would* be Hell." She groaned. "I'm sorry. This is way too heavy for Christmas night. Where were we before all this?"

"You were saying that you were afraid you might fall for me."

"Before that."

"Before that, you were talking about how sweet I am."

"Even before that."

I leaned into her and we kissed.

CHAPTER

Forty-Three

How quickly the fantasy of Christmas passes.

✦ Luke Crisp's Diary ✦

I woke the next morning exhausted. I hadn't gotten home from Rachael's until after two in the morning, so I skipped my usual exercise and stopped to get bagels. On the way there I went to call Rachael when I noticed that my cell phone was missing. *Must have fallen out on Rachael's couch,* I thought. The thought made me smile. I was excited to see her.

I bought a half dozen bagels with a tub of strawberry-flavored cream cheese and carried them into the copy shop. I was surprised that Rachael's car wasn't in the parking lot.

"Merry Christmas," I said as I walked in through the back door.

"Hey," Colby said weakly. His eyes were dull and he was frowning.

"Hey, yourself. What's wrong, run out of eggnog? Have a bagel."

He just stared at me with a sad expression. "You haven't heard, have you?"

"Heard what?"

"You better talk to Wayne."

I set the bagels down on the back counter and walked into

Wayne's office. To my surprise he was on his knees emptying his desk into a cardboard box.

"What are you doing?" I asked.

He looked up at me. "Congratulations," he said. "You've been promoted."

"I know. We already celebrated that."

"You've been promoted again. You're the new store manager."

I just stood there. "Is this a joke?"

"I wish," he said. "I got a message this morning that my employment has been terminated. I guess they didn't want to do it before Christmas, so they waited for the day after."

"This doesn't make any sense."

"It did to someone at corporate."

"What grounds did they give you?"

"Sales have fallen."

"Everyone's sales have fallen. The whole economy has fallen."

He stopped what he was doing and looked at me. "That's just the legal reason. The real reason I've been let go is that I'm just eighteen months from collecting my pension. Firing me will save the company a lot of money."

"They would never do that," I said.

"Carl Crisp would never do that. But he doesn't run the company anymore. It's that new guy, Price." He slammed a drawer shut. "By the way, they also let Rachael go."

"Rachael? Why?"

"She's an insurance liability," he said. "Her son's medical bills are more than the rest of ours combined."

"Does she know yet?"

"I called her an hour ago."

As I watched Wayne fill his box, it suddenly occurred to me what was going on. "They're dumping ballast," I said.

"What?"

"They're dumping ballast. Crisp's is dropping liabilities. They're getting ready to cash out the company." I shook my head. "Wayne, this is my fault."

Wayne laughed darkly. "Luke, you may have your faults, but this is one even you can't claim."

"I wish that were true," I said. "Henry Price took over the company when Carl retired. He wasn't supposed to."

"Who was?" Wayne asked.

"Me."

He stood, staring at me blankly. I could see in his eyes when it came to him. "You're Carl's son."

I nodded. "I *was*."

"What do you mean, *was*?"

I raked my hair back with both hands. "My father wanted me to take over the company. Instead, I took my million-dollar trust fund and ran off to Europe and squandered it all. He's disowned me."

Wayne stood there silently for a moment. "The Carl I know would never disown his son."

"I think I know him a little better than you do."

"No doubt. But I know him better than you think. And you could be mistaken." He leaned back against his desk.

"When Crisp's was first starting out, they were quickly expanding into new markets. This location was the first store in Nevada. One of your father's new managers, a former car salesman, was given the chance to pitch the MGM account. It was worth more than a million dollars a year in business.

"The manager went into the meeting acting like the cocky car salesman that he was. He didn't even talk about MGM or their needs, he talked only about himself. Not surprisingly, they practically threw him out of their office and gave their business to someone else.

"It was a big defeat for Crisp's. Your father flew in to personally meet with MGM and then the copy center's manager and staff. The manager, rightfully, was certain that your father had come to fire him. Instead, your father took him aside and asked him what happened. The manager admitted that he'd handled the meeting poorly. Then your father asked him what he'd learned from the experience. The manager told him, 'Humility. The opportunity to pitch an account is a privilege. It's much more important to listen than to talk.'

"Your father said, 'Good. Don't make that mistake again.' Then he turned to go. As he was about to leave, the manager said, 'You're not firing me?' Your father said, 'Are you kidding? I just spent a million dollars on your education.' Twenty years later that man is still with Crisp's."

"Sounds like company legend," I said.

"It is a legend," Wayne said. "But it's true. That idiot car salesman was me." He nodded slowly. "If your father stood by me, a stupid, brash, former car salesman, he would never stop believing in you. Your father is a man of integrity. What's going on now would never have happened if he hadn't handed over the reins."

"I was supposed to be holding those reins," I said. "This never would have happened if I had done the right thing. Now you and Rachael and good employees across America are paying for my failure." I put both hands on my head. "How many others have I hurt?" I walked to the door. "I'm going to fix this, Wayne. No one is going to suffer anymore because of me."

"What are you going to do?"

"I'm going to Phoenix to talk to Henry Price."

CHAPTER

Forty-Four

How quickly the fates can mess with our lives.

✦ Luke Crisp's Diary ✦

From Crisp's I drove directly to Rachael's house. *With no job and no insurance, she must be terrified*, I thought. I needed to talk to her. I needed to tell her that I was going to fix this. I needed to tell her that everything would be all right.

I ran up to her apartment and knocked on her door. I had seen her car in the parking lot, so I was surprised that she didn't answer. *Open up.* I knocked again. This time the door partially opened, just enough for Rachael to look through the crack at me. Her face was stained with tears.

"Rachael, I'm so sorry about what happened," I said. "I'm going to . . ."

"Get out of here," she said.

"What?"

"I don't ever want to see you again."

"I don't understand. I just found out about your job, I didn't . . ."

"You lied to me."

"Rachael," I said. "What are you talking about?"

"You're a liar!" she screamed. "You said you lost your money on the stock market. You lost it gambling."

"That's not true," I said.

"Quit lying to me! I read your text," she said. "Do you want me to read it?" She held up my cell phone and read from it. "Luke, gambling losses are only tax deductible from winnings. No refund on two hundred seventy-two thousand seven hundred forty-seven dollars and thirty-two cents." She looked back up at me. "You knew what had happened to me. How could you lie to me about that?" She threw my phone out into the hallway. "All I wanted was a little honesty!" She began to sob. "Why did you have to lie to me? I really cared about you."

She slammed her door shut and locked it. I knocked. "Rachael," I said. "I can explain."

Nothing. I bent over and picked up my phone and read the text message myself. Mike Semken had selected a remarkably bad time to respond to the tax question I'd sent weeks earlier.

I put my ear against her door. I could hear her crying inside. "Please, Rachael."

I knocked on her door for what seemed a half hour before I finally gave up. She wasn't going to talk to me.

CHAPTER

Forty-Five

*I've seen newspaper photographs of disaster sites
after a tornado has blown through,
destroying entire neighborhoods in mere seconds.
That's what my world feels like.*

✦ Luke Crisp's Diary ✦

Even as heartsick as I was, there was still something I needed to do. Not just for Wayne, but for Rachael and good people like them around the country. Whatever it took, I had to get their jobs back.

I got in my car and started off for Phoenix. I didn't blame Rachael for being so upset. After what she'd suffered through with her husband, I understood why she would be panicked about what she'd read. I probably would be too. I just needed a chance to explain things. It had been so difficult getting her to open up in the first place I wondered if I would ever get that chance.

Scottsdale is a little more than 300 miles from Las Vegas, nearly a straight shot southeast on Highway 93, a five-hour drive if you do the limit—four and a half hours if you're motivated. I made it to Phoenix by late afternoon. I drove directly to the Crisp's headquarters and took the elevator to the seventh floor, where my father's office used to be. I hardly recognized it. The furniture in the waiting room was different: sleek, new and showy—as was the young woman sitting at the reception desk.

"I'm here to see Henry," I said.

She looked at me dully. "Do you have an appointment?"

"I don't need one," I said. "Tell him Luke Crisp is here."

"Luke who?"

"Crisp, as in Crisp's Copy Centers." When she didn't say anything, I added, "The company you work for."

"Does Mr. Price know what this is regarding?"

"Just get him," I said impatiently.

She picked up her phone and pressed a button. I heard her say my name in hushed tones. A moment later she said, "Mr. Price won't be available to meet with you until tomorrow afternoon."

"He'll meet with me now," I said, walking past her. I walked down the hallway into Henry's office. Henry was on the phone and glanced up at me with a surprised, unhappy expression. My father's office had changed as well, the new décor resembling the modern motif of the reception area. Even Henry looked different. He wore an expensive-looking jacket with a black T-shirt underneath.

"Henry," I said.

He held up a finger to silence me. "Just a minute," he said into the phone. "I just had someone barge into my office. No problem, I'll call you right back. You too." He returned the phone to its cradle, his eyes never leaving me. "Luke, what a surprise. What brings you back to the Grand Canyon State?"

"I need to talk to you about the changes you're making at Crisp's."

He leaned back in his chair, his fingers knit together on top of his desk. "What changes would you be referring to?"

"Firing your lifelong employees before they can get their pensions, to begin with."

"I'm not firing people so they'll lose their pensions. I'm only releasing those who aren't keeping pace."

"That's a lie, Henry. The company's down across the board because the entire economy is down."

"Which is why someone needs to make the tough decisions that are right for the company."

"My father would never do it this way."

"You're right, but your father doesn't run Crisp's anymore, Luke. This is my show now."

The way he said this sounded mutinous, as if he'd thrown my father from the ship. "You're making a mistake, Henry."

"Says who? The Crisp's pension plan was a mistake to begin with. You said so yourself. There's no tangible return on investment."

"No return on investment? How about employee satisfaction and retention?"

Henry grinned. "We don't need long-term employees to make money. We're a copy company, not NASA. Most of our people could be replaced by trained monkeys."

"What about *loyalty*?" I said.

"What about *profits*?" he replied. "That's why corporations exist. Or don't they teach that at Wharton anymore?" He leaned back in his chair. "So what's your angle, Luke? You suddenly care about this because . . ."

"I'm not here for me. I'm here for the people I work with."

He looked at me quizzically. "The people you work with."

Suddenly his eyes lit. "Wait. You're not telling me that you're working for Crisp's."

"Store 317 in Las Vegas."

"Wow, that is . . . poetic. The prodigal son gets his due." He groaned with amusement.

"Henry, please don't hurt these people who trusted in *us*. The decisions you're making are hurting the people who built this company."

"What's this 'us'? You're not part of this, Luke. The Crisp name is a trademark, nothing more. And the decisions your father was making were hurting people—the people he was morally and ethically obligated to protect. They're called shareholders. And if the employees don't like it, they can work elsewhere. Remember what you said to me not so long ago, 'We're not a charity.' "

"I was wrong about a lot of things back then."

"Well, that's true, but irrelevant."

"You were hoping all along that I would leave, weren't you?"

"Also true but irrelevant." He glanced down at his watch. "It's good to see you again, Luke, but I've got to run. The Suns are playing tonight." He pushed a button on his intercom. "Brandi, please have security escort Mr. Crisp out of the building."

"Don't bother," I said. I turned to walk out.

"Luke," Henry said.

I turned around.

"You can't fight karma."

I looked at his stupid, grinning face, then walked out of the office.

✦

I knew what I had to do even before I got to my car. There was no other way. As difficult as it would be, I had no choice. I had to face my father.

CHAPTER

Forty-Six

I am facing the most difficult thing of my life—
my own greatest failure.

✦ Luke Crisp's Diary ✦

I sat in the car in front of my father's house for nearly an hour gathering my thoughts or courage, I'm not sure which. Then again, maybe I was just stalling. I feared facing my father more than anyone or anything I could ever remember. *I was dead to him.* Those words Henry had pronounced continued to echo in my conscience. My guilt was searing. I couldn't imagine how much I must have hurt my father to make him pronounce my death. My father was as generous and good as anyone I had ever met, but he could also be austere and sharp-tongued. My father didn't tolerate fools—and I was a fool of the worst sort. Honestly, I don't think I would have knocked on his door if my visit was only for myself. But it wasn't. I'd come for people I cared about more than myself. I hoped he would listen to me. I hoped I would have the chance to say what I needed to say before he threw me out.

I walked up the front cobblestone walk and stood on the doorstep. Then, before I could reconsider, reached out and pushed the doorbell. It felt odd, ringing the bell to the house I had grown up in—a door I had slammed a million times after school.

It seemed like an eternity before the door opened to a middle-aged woman I did not know. "May I help you?" she asked. But before I could speak the woman's eyes narrowed. "You're Luke."

I wondered who she was. I wondered where Mary was.

"I'm here to see my father," I said. "Tell him I won't stay long."

She looked at me a moment more, then stepped back. "I'll tell your father that you're here."

She walked away and I stepped into the foyer. Somehow the home seemed foreign to me—the familiarity was gone. *How could it be gone?* Maybe it wasn't. Maybe it was something inside of me that was gone. When she didn't return, I began to doubt that he would see me. As the minutes passed, I was sure of it. Of course he wouldn't. I was dead to him. *The dead are best kept buried.*

As I was wondering what I should do, the woman walked back into the foyer. "Your father's in his den."

I mumbled a terse thank you, then walked down the hall past the dining room. The hallway outside my father's den was always dim. I slowly opened the door. The room was also dark, lit only by desk or floor lamps, illuminating the room in places.

Then I saw him. On the opposite side of the room, on the other side of his desk, my father sat in his tall, throne-like chair. His hair was thin and gray, and for a moment the two of us just looked at each other. My father's eyes were locked on mine—those sharp, piercing eyes, dark and unreadable.

I stepped inside. "Sir . . ."

He held up a finger, silencing me. He just stared at me for a moment then he said, "Are you really here?"

My mouth felt dry. "I'm sorry, I just . . ." I took a step toward him, desperately wanting to hide from him and knowing I couldn't. "I've come to apologize." I dropped my head. "You were right to disown me. I'm so sorry." I put my head down, waiting for his words—his rebuke and rejection. It didn't come. Then I heard something. I heard a sniff. I looked up. My father's eyes were red. He didn't speak because he was crying.

"My boy," he said softly. "My boy." Tears flowed freely down his face. He stood, walking around his desk with his arms stretched out to me. "My boy!"

"Dad?"

"Mary!" he shouted. "Mary! Luke has come home! My son has come home!"

He walked forward and we embraced, his still powerful arms nearly crushing me. I began to sob. I couldn't look into his face. "I'm sorry. I'm so sorry."

My father just held me, kissing my head. "I've prayed every night that you would find your way back. And you've come back. You came back. It's all that matters."

Just then Mary stepped inside the room. She froze when she saw me. "Luke!"

"He's back, Mary!"

Her eyes immediately welled up with tears. She walked over and hugged me. "I told you he would come back, didn't I?"

"You never lost faith." He pulled me still tighter. "My boy. Oh, my boy." He said to Mary, "Make reservations at DiSera's. Tell Larry to hold our table. Tell Larry to pour the Monfortino and break out his mandolin. We're celebrating. My boy's come home."

CHAPTER

Forty-Seven

The sweetness of reunion is the joy of Heaven.

✦ Luke Crisp's Diary ✦

There we were. The two of us (actually three of us, since Mary had come), sitting at the same table where we'd sat when my father had first suggested that I go off to school. The joy I felt was indescribable. Yet, it was my father who seemed most joyful. My father was positively giddy, as if he might suddenly burst into song.

The Monfortino wine we drank was special not just because it was DiSera's best, but at $1,000 a bottle, it was something my father had never ordered—would never order. But tonight he did. It was a gesture, and it wasn't lost on me. Tonight, nothing was held back.

My father wanted to know everything about what I'd been through. Everything. I told him about our journey, my extravagances and partying. I was embarrassed to confess my foolishness, but my father just listened and shook his head knowingly. When I told him about Sean and how he had taken me, his only comment was "I've been there."

His eyes welled up with tears when I told him about Candace leaving me, more when I told him about the months I spent under the Las Vegas streets and even more when I told him about being mugged. His eyes shone with gratitude when I told him about Carlos and how he had saved me. He smiled when I told him about Wayne.

"I remember Wayne," my father said. "He looks like Gepetto in the Disney cartoon."

I laughed. "That's him."

"He really screwed up that MGM bid," he said, grinning. He sighed and took a drink of wine. "Every now and then I do something right."

When I told him about Rachael, I realized how much she meant to me.

"It's not done, is it?" my father said.

I shook my head. "Not yet."

Throughout my story my father never once reprimanded me. There was no judgment. No "I told you so." No anger. Only love and joy at my return.

Later in the evening, after Larry had finished playing *Volare* for us on his mandolin, my father stood up and clinked his fork against his wineglass until everyone in the restaurant was looking at us.

"My friends," he said. "Most of you are strangers. But tonight, you are all my friends—because tonight we are celebrating. My son has come home. I invite you all to join me in a toast."

Larry walked around his restaurant, gesturing wildly and shouting "Glasses up!" Larry's restaurant was his home and he ran it as such. (He was notorious for throwing out people he didn't like, which only added to his restaurant's fame and popularity.)

Even without Larry's encouragement, most of the restaurant's occupants were already smiling and raising their glasses. *Who doesn't love a happy reunion?*

My father lifted his glass. "To my son. Wherever he has sailed, I give thanks to the winds that brought him home."

We touched our glasses as my eyes filled with tears. Such gratitude and love filled my heart for this man. For *his* love.

My father looked out over the dining room. "Thank you for sharing our joy," my father said. "Tonight, your dinners are all on me." The entire restaurant broke out into applause. Then Mary whispered something to him and he grinned wryly. "But not your drinks."

Everyone laughed, then applauded again.

"*Cantiamo!*" Larry shouted. "We sing." He played *That's Amore* on his mandolin and the entire restaurant sang like we were old friends. Everyone except my father. The whole time my father just looked at me and smiled.

CHAPTER

Forty-Eight

My return has awoken the giant.

 Luke Crisp's Diary ✦

The next morning, Henry's secretary looked at me narrowly, clearly annoyed to see me back in her office so soon. "May I help you?" she asked in a tone that left no doubt that she had no intention of doing so.

"Yes, you may. Please tell Henry that I'm here to see him."

"Mr. Price is busy," she snapped.

"He's not too busy to see me," I replied. "Call him."

She didn't move.

"Please call him," I repeated.

She glared at me as she lifted her phone and spoke into it. Then she returned the phone to its cradle. "Like I said, he's busy. And you're not welcome here."

My father stepped up to the desk. "That's okay, miss. I'll clear his schedule." He started past her desk.

"You can't go back there. I'll call security."

My father stopped and turned back, looking at her with a bemused smile. "My dear, security is already on its way."

Almost as if on cue, three uniformed security men walked into the room. They crossed the room to my father. The first one said, "It's good to see you again, Mr. Crisp."

"You too, Michael," my father said. My father turned back to the woman, "You have no idea who I am, do you?"

She looked at my father, speechless.

"You don't, do you?"

She swallowed, then shook her head.

"I thought as much," he said. "I'll tell you who I'm not. I'm no longer your employer." He turned to one of the guards. "Michael, will one of your men please escort this young lady from my building."

"Yes, sir," Michael said, nodding to the man next to him.

My father continued on to Henry's office. I stopped at the woman's desk. "Word of advice," I said. "If you intend to keep a job in the future, you should really get to know who you work for."

My dad tried Henry's door but it was locked, no doubt due to my last intrusion. He knocked on the door.

"I don't have time for you, Luke," Henry shouted.

"Would you have time for me, Henry?" my father asked.

Silence. Suddenly the door opened. "Carl. My apologies, I thought that . . ."

"I was my son?" My father walked into the office. "Take a seat, Henry."

"Yes, sir." Henry scurried back to his desk.

My father looked around at his old office. "What have you been doing with my office, Henry?"

Henry swallowed. "A few changes here and there. Just making it mine."

"Clearly," my father said. He turned back to Henry. "What have you been doing with my company, Henry?"

Henry forced a nervous smile. "I've been streamlining it, sir."

"Streamlining?"

"Yes, sir. Throwing out the waste."

"Good," my father said, "I hate waste." He walked over to the wall and looked at a picture of Henry standing on stage with a rap star. "What is this?"

"We brought a rapper in to our last conference. I thought it would build morale."

"Did you now?" My father took the picture off the wall. "Like I said, I hate waste." He dropped the picture in the garbage can near the desk. "I'm going to help you, Henry. We're going to streamline things a little more." My father turned back. "As of this moment, you're relieved of your duties."

Henry looked at my father in shock. "But, Carl. Please. I was just taking care of the shareholders."

"Have you forgotten that I am the majority shareholder?"

"No, sir."

"I think you have." He leaned forward, his powerful eyes blazing. For a moment I thought he might throttle Henry, who looked absolutely terrified. "You've forgotten the principles of this company, Henry—that I can forgive you for. You've betrayed the people who built this company—that I can almost forgive you for. But you disrespected my son, Henry. That I will not forgive you for." He turned back to the two remaining security guards who stood in the hallway. "Michael, see Mr. Price from my building. He is no longer welcome here."

"Yes, sir."

"And Henry," my father said.

Henry looked at him pensively.

"You can't fight karma." My father turned back to me and winked. "Let's go, son. We've got work to do."

CHAPTER

Forty-Nine

My father has asked to meet those who helped me in my hard times.
Returning to Las Vegas has filled me with peculiar emotions.
I feel like the actor who returns to the stage
of an empty theater when the show is through,
or the soldier who visits the battlefield years after the war has ended.

✦ Luke Crisp's Diary ✦

The black Lincoln looked out of place in front of the adobe ranch house. The driver put the car in park and turned off the ignition.

"This is the place," I said.

"Then let's go," my father said. As usual, he stepped out of the car before the driver could open his door. I climbed out after him and we walked together to the front door of the Sanchez home. Carlos had seen the car pull up outside and opened the door before we got to it. He looked back and forth between my father and me.

"Hi, Carlos. This is my father," I said, even though I thought he'd probably already figured that out.

"It's an honor, sir."

"It's mine," my father said. "May we come in for a moment?"

"Of course."

As we stepped into the home's living room, Carmen walked into the room. "Luke!" she said. She hugged me, then turned to my father. "Are you Luke's father?"

"Yes, I'm Carl," he said. "May I have a seat?"

"Of course," Carlos said, motioning to a faded, green velvet-upholstered armchair near the center of the room. "Please, sit."

My father sat down on the edge of the chair, while Carlos and Carmen sat next to each other on a sofa just a few yards in front of him. I sat on a smaller upholstered chair to the side.

My father looked down for a moment as he gathered his thoughts, then up at Carlos. "I came to thank you for saving my boy."

"I didn't really. He . . ."

My father stopped him. "Luke's told me everything. You were there when my son needed you. I'd like to repay the favor. I understand your oldest son is ill. Tell me about it."

Carlos glanced over at Carmen, then back at my father. "He has cardiomyopathy," he said. "It's a disease of the heart."

"A very serious disease," my father said. He turned to Carmen. "How is he doing?"

"He's still with us," Carmen said.

My father looked at them for a moment. "I'd like to keep it that way. A golf buddy of mine, Dr. Marion Nelson, is the head of cardiology at St. Joseph's Hospital in Phoenix. I've told him about your son's condition and he's prepared to admit him at any time."

Carlos and Carmen looked a little uneasy. "Thank you, sir," Carlos said, "but my son doesn't have insurance."

"Everything's taken care of," my father said. "It's on my tab."

The two of them stared at my father in disbelief. I knew that my father wanted to personally thank them, but I had known nothing about the extent of his plan. I looked at my father and smiled. Then my father stood. He took two business cards from inside his coat pocket and handed them to Carlos. "That's the doctor's card and mine. He's expecting your call. All your son needs to do is make an appointment and show up."

Carmen burst out in tears. "Bless you!"

Carlos also began to cry. He and Carmen hugged, then Carlos said to my father, "Thank you. Thank you, Mr. Crisp. Thank you."

"Carl," my father said, smiling. "The gratitude is mine. If Dr. Nelson says your son can fly, just call my assistant and I'll have her book your flight and arrange a car to take you to the medical center." He looked over at me and smiled. My eyes were now also filled with tears and I nodded my approval.

"Shall we go, son?"

"Yes, sir."

Carlos and Carmen walked us out to the front walk. Carlos kept looking down at the cards and Carmen kept hugging me. "Someone pinch me," Carmen said. "God bless you, Carl. God bless you."

"He has," my father said.

Once we were in the car, I said to my father, "You didn't tell me that you were going to do that."

A broad, almost childish grin crossed his face. "Fun, wasn't it?"

I nodded. "Yes it was."

The driver looked back at us. "The airport, sir?"

"No," my father said. "There's one more thing I need to see."

CHAPTER

*The changing seasons of circumstance
can melt away stretches of our lives
like frost in the warmth of spring.
This was my last December.*

✦ Luke Crisp's Diary ✦

My father and I stood above the concrete embankment looking down into the mouth of the flood tunnel.

"You lived in there?" he asked softly.

"Home sweet home," I said. "About a hundred yards in from the entrance, I made myself a cozy little cardboard nest."

My father was quiet as he looked down at the tunnel, and I wondered what was going through his mind. Then, after a minute or so, he asked, "What did you learn, son?"

I looked down into the gulley for a moment, then back at him. "I learned to be grateful."

He nodded and I could tell that my answer pleased him. "Anything else?"

A large smile crossed my face. "I learned that my father's love was unfaltering."

His eyes welled up. "Unfaltering, unconditional, unceasing." He turned and looked at me, his eyes focused on mine. "Never, ever, ever forget that." He put his arm around me. "Are you ready to go home?"

"Almost," I said. "Almost."

CHAPTER

Fifty-One

*I don't know what's behind the curtain,
only that I need to find out.*

✦ Luke Crisp's Diary ✦

My father turned to me as I got out of the car in front of Crisp's. "I haven't been to 317 for nearly twenty years."

"It's a good center," I said. "Wayne's done a good job."

"Wayne's done an exceptional job. His store is ranked second in volume in Nevada and twelfth in the western region."

"How do you keep all these figures in your head?" I asked.

"You'll get the hang of it," he replied.

I opened the door for my father, then followed him in. Colby greeted us as we walked inside. "Luke!"

Colby reminded me of a puppy. If he had a tail, it would be wagging. "Colby!"

"I didn't know if you were coming back."

"You think I'd leave without saying goodbye?"

"Nah."

I looked around. "Is Rachael here?"

He shook his head. "No. She hasn't come back yet. Wayne can't get a hold of her." He suddenly looked at my father with a peculiar expression, and I suspected that he was wondering if my father really was who he thought he was. He turned back to me. "Hey, did Wayne know that you were coming?"

"No," I said, as my father and I walked around the counter. "We thought we'd surprise him." We walked back to Wayne's office. His door was shut and I knocked on it.

"Come in," he said.

I opened the door. "Anybody home?" I said. Wayne was eating lunch at his desk. His face lit up when he saw me. "Luke!"

I opened the door the rest of the way. "Hey, buddy."

He stood up and walked to me, extending his hand. "It's so good to see you. I can't believe you did it. How did you get Price to change his mind?"

"I didn't," I said.

He looked at me quizzically. "Huh?"

Just then my father walked into the doorway. Wayne immediately stiffened, like an enlisted man standing at attention for an officer. My father smiled at his reaction. "At ease, soldier," he said. My father put out his hand. "How are you, Wayne?"

"Mr. Crisp. I'm terrific, thank you." They shook.

"It's been how many years since we had our talk here?"

"Twenty-three and a half. Give or take a few months."

"You were a good investment. You've done a great job with this store. Congratulations."

"Thank you."

"No, thank you. And especially for taking such good care of my son. He speaks highly of you."

"He's a good man. You should be proud of him," Wayne said. "A chip off the old block."

"I am proud of him," he said looking at me. "Always have been."

"Wayne," I said, "do you know where Rachael is?"

"No. I haven't been able to reach her. She's not answering her phone. I planned to drive by her place this afternoon to see if I could catch her."

"So she still doesn't know she has her job back."

He shook his head. "No."

"We'll visit her," my father said. "I'll let her know."

Wayne smiled. "I'm sure she won't be expecting that."

My father and Wayne visited a little while longer and then we went back to the car. On the way over to Rachael's apartment my father asked, "So, Luke. What's your plan?"

"My plan?"

"Your plan to win back the girl."

"Honesty," I said.

"And if that doesn't work?"

"Beg."

He laughed. "How much do you care about this woman?"

"I'm not sure how to quantify that."

He smiled. "Have you stopped thinking about her since you last saw her?"

"No."

"Is she the one?"

"I'm not sure." Then I added, "But I'd really like the chance to find out."

He sat back in the leather seat and looked forward again. "That's what I wanted to know. You better let me handle this."

Rachael's car was parked in her reserved space at the apartment building. The driver parked below the apartment's west entrance, and my father and I went inside the building and up to the second floor.

"It's 207," I said.

My father walked up to the door while I stood down the hall where she couldn't see me. My father knocked on her door. A moment later I heard the locks slide, then the door open.

"May I help you?" Rachael asked. Hearing her voice made me both happy and nervous.

"You're Rachael Simmons?" my father asked.

"Yes," she said. Long pause. "You look like . . ."

My father reached out his hand. "I'm Carl Crisp. I'm the founder of Crisp's Copy Centers. I'm here because I was mortified by some of the actions that were taken in my absence—actions that included the termination of some valued employees, you being one of them. I came on behalf of myself and Crisp's Copy Centers, to extend an apology and offer you back your job."

She was temporarily speechless. "Are you doing this with everyone?"

My father laughed. "No."

"Thank you," she said, her voice piqued with emotion. "You don't know how much this means to me."

"I might." His gaze intensified. "Rachael, do you like my company?"

"A lot more today," she said.

My father laughed.

"I think it's a great company," she said. "You've always taken good care of your employees."

"I'm glad you said that, because I think we can do an even better job of taking care of you. I'd like to make you an offer. We have a position available in our corporate office. You would keep all your benefits but your salary would be substantially more. You would also be able to work from home in the afternoons so you could be there when your son gets home from school."

I desperately wanted to see her face.

"There are, however, a couple catches."

"Like what?"

"The first is that you would, of course, have to move to Phoenix."

"I have no problem with that," she said quickly.

"The second is not as pleasant. You would have to answer directly to Crisp's new CEO."

"Why would I have a problem with that?" she asked.

"Well, I think you better find out who he is first." My father turned and gestured me forward. I walked up to the door. Rachael froze when she saw me. She still didn't know that he was my father, and she looked back and forth between us, trying to understand the connection.

"This is my son, Luke. He is likely to be Crisp's new CEO."

Rachael just stared at me.

My father said, "I would consider it a personal favor if you would at least listen to what he has to say." He looked at me, then back at Rachael. "I'll give you some time alone. It's a pleasure meeting you, Rachael." He turned to me. "The floor is yours, son."

He walked back down the hall and disappeared down the stairwell. Rachael stood there staring at me.

"Hi," I said.

She threw her arms around me. "I never thought I'd see you again."

I put my arms around her and pulled her close.

"I'm sorry I wouldn't let you explain," she said. "I was so afraid. And I wanted you to be good. I wanted it so bad."

"I don't gamble," I said.

"I know. I called your accountant."

"Mike told you?"

"I told him it was a matter of life or death," she said.

I held her for several minutes. When she finally leaned back, she said to me with a grin, "So you've *met* Mr. Crisp, have you?"

"I'm sorry. *That* I was hiding from you."

"I'll forgive you," she said, falling back into me.

"So what's the verdict?" I asked. "Will you come to Phoenix?"

She smiled. "What do you think?"

EPILOGUE

*My father once said, "The warrior who goes off to battle
should not boast as the one who returns from it."
I realize now that I have only to boast of good people
who held my shield when my arms were too weak,
and lifted me up when I was too tired to stand on my own.*

✦ Luke Crisp's Diary ✦

My father and I are back to golfing every Saturday. I'd golf more if I could, but I'm a bit tied down to my new responsibilities: the board voted unanimously to install me as the new CEO of Crisp's Copy Centers International. The truth is, my father has enough voting shares that he could have done it without their approval, but that's not his style. Never has been. I'm now working on expanding Crisp's into Europe, so my travels through France and Italy weren't a complete waste. The last time I went to Paris, I took Rachael with me. We had a really good time.

In response to my father's question, it turns out that Rachael was the one after all. We were married on December 22nd, a year from the night we talked in the coffee shop. Of course the wedding dinner was held at DiSera's and we were serenaded by Larry, who announced to all that he'd never seen such a beautiful bride. I agreed. Sure, it could just be the rose-tinted lenses of love, but I think not. I think happiness makes everyone more beautiful.

My father was overjoyed to become an instant grandfather and, in his usual way of approaching life, jumped headfirst into the role. He's now teaching Chris to golf and spends every Sunday afternoon with his grandson. Seeing my father with Chris reminds me of when I was a boy. Chris isn't going to counseling anymore. In fact, he's doing great. Of course he is. He's got my dad.

Henry Price left Phoenix to start his own chain of copy centers. He opened his first store in the St. Paul area and never grew past that. I learned from our Twin City associates that Henry's copy center just limped along for a few years until his capital ran out and the investors pulled the plug. I guess he learned that my father really did know something about business after all.

Duane had his heart surgery. Tasha and Carmen stayed at my father's house as Duane recovered. The operation was successful and Tasha's now pregnant with their third child. Carmen can't look at my father without bursting into tears. She calls him St. Carl and I think she means it. Of course I feel the same way about her Carlos. Carlos is still managing the Golden Age and calls occasionally for marketing advice. I'm always glad to hear from him.

The Wharton 7 was scattered to the wind. I haven't seen Sean since that day at the Rehab, and I'm fine with that. My attorneys filed suit against both him and Marshall and I received a judgment against both. Marshall paid what he owed me—but Sean still hasn't. I'm not holding my breath.

I don't know what's become of Suzie, but I talked to Lucy a few years ago. She had her baby—a little boy, Brandon—who was now walking. She met an older man in her aunt's church. They got married and settled down in Thornton, Colorado, a suburb of Denver.

Before she hung up, she told me that she had heard from Candace. Candace had married a Boston neurosurgeon and now lives in Duxbury. Lucy said she had asked about me. Honestly, I have no hard feelings toward her. If she hadn't left me, I wouldn't have my Rachael. Thank God for unanswered prayers.

That's about the whole of it—at least from my side of the story. The pages continue to turn, and every day I'm a little older, hopefully a little wiser and a lot more grateful. Do I have regrets? I have a few—but not as many as you might think. If it hadn't been for the darkness, I never would have known the light. In life we all take different paths, some more difficult than others, but in the end, all that matters is whether or not they lead us home.

At the beginning of this story I wrote that people oftentimes misunderstand the word "prodigal"—thinking it means "lost" or "wayward," when it really means *wastefully extravagant*.

But there is another meaning to the word—one rarely used—but correct all the same. Prodigal also means "to give abundantly." And in this sense, even more than me, my father was the truest of prodigals. He still is. He is my hero, my champion, and my savior. My greatest wish is to be like him. My greatest hope is to be worthy to be called his son. I don't think I could aspire to anything greater than that.

ichard Paul Evans is the #1 best-selling author of *The Christmas Box* and *Michael Vey*. His eighteen novels have each appeared on the *New York Times* best-seller list; there are more than 14 million copies of his books in print. His books have been translated into more than twenty-two languages and several have been international best-sellers. He is the winner of the 1998 American Mothers Book Award, two first-place *Storytelling World* Awards for his children's books, the 2005 *Romantic Times* Best Women's Novel of the Year Award, the 2010 Leserpreis-Gold Award for Romance and the 2011 Wilbur Award for fiction. Evans received the *Washington Times* Humanitarian of the Century Award and the Volunteers of America National Empathy Award for his work helping abused children. Evans lives in Salt Lake City, Utah, with his wife, Keri, and their five children.

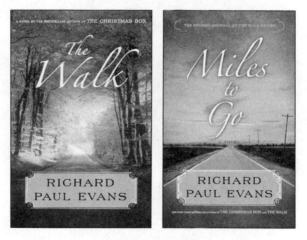

Are you missing out?
Join Richard Paul Evans on Richard's Facebook Author Page.

Richard himself contributes almost daily.

Richard's page has fun facts, great contests, first peeks, deep thoughts, GratiTuesday, and just about everything you want to know about one of America's most beloved authors. When you join this thriving community you'll get to know Richard like you never dreamed possible. Join us today!

It's easy to join.

1. Login to Facebook
2. Type Richard Paul Evans in search
3. Click on Richard Paul Evans Author (or Writer)
4. Click on LIKE. Welcome!

Or write to him at P.O. Box 712137
Salt Lake City, Utah 84171